COUGAR PROWLS

Battle-hardened Carroll Cougar has finally made it home to his little ranch on Twin Creek with his new bride, Ellen, after spending years fighting under General Crook in the Apache Wars. But Cougar and Ellen have left too many enemies alive behind them, and more have accumulated in Twin Creek in their absence. Once more, Cougar must buckle on his guns and go out prowling, until he has defeated every last one of his adversaries.

OWEN G. IRONS

COUGAR PROWLS

Complete and Unabridged

LINFORD
Leicester

First published in Great Britain in 2014 by
Robert Hale Limited
London

First Linford Edition
published 2017
by arrangement with
Robert Hale
an imprint of
The Crowood Press
Wiltshire

A catalogue record for this book is available
from the British Library.

ISBN 978–1–4448–3486–4

Published by
F. A. Thorpe (Publishing)
Anstey, Leicestershire

Set by Words & Graphics Ltd.
Anstey, Leicestershire
Printed and bound in Great Britain by
T. J. International Ltd., Padstow, Cornwall

This book is printed on acid-free paper

1

Cougar still had Reineke's small force in sight, but with the spread of open desert ahead of him, there was little he could do to close the distance between them unseen. They were heading south again now and there were only so many trails ahead of them entering the red-green hills where they would be traveling toward the higher peaks of the White Mountains.

Sycamore Creek trail ran that way, but why would they be riding Sycamore Creek? His first guess would be that Reineke would strike out across the playa flats toward Fort Apache, but he was obviously wrong in that guess.

For now he could only trail along in their dust, following them until the chance to strike against Reineke offered itself.

Reineke had dropped two men back

to serve as drag scouts. Cougar had smiled to himself as he watched them split from the group and circle slowly back in his direction through the brushy canyons. Reineke hadn't forgotten everything that he knew.

What was it, he wondered, that had caused Solon Reineke to turn bad? After the violent rape and murder of Carlina Polk, the girl Cougar had intended to marry, it was all too obvious that there was something not quite human in Solon Reineke, something none of them, least of all Cougar, had recognized before. But now Solon had become totally treacherous and unstable, focused only on evil, it seemed. He was a traitor now to his own country, willing to assassinate General Crook in the name of a foreign government, for power, glory and gold. Himself creating an ambitious plan to create a new Indian nation in the southwest. The Apaches, the Comanches and some of the Kiowa bands had agreed to fight with Reineke.

Additionally, Reineke had convinced

men in Mexico, always desirous of regaining the lands there, to assist him. Foreign adventurists, primarily the Prussians, had likely been told that the time was right for them to establish new colonies. None of this could ever work, of course — the varying factions could never establish common agreement. But they were agreed that the Americans must be driven out, and as a sign of this white's — Reineke's — dedicated intentions, he would assassinate the American general, George Crook — that was to be the signal for a general Indian uprising. Reineke meant to let the other factions fight it out while he established his own new country across the broad desert lands.

How did a man go so very twisted and wrong?

The man who unknowingly had fallen back to flank Cougar on the right had ridden into a little twisted gorge where the willow brush, greening from the recent rain, caused him tough going.

Cougar sighed. The man, unfortunately, was in his way.

He had no wish to kill absolute strangers, even if they were foreign soldiers on American soil, but that was obviously what they meant to do to him if he let them. Cougar turned the buckskin upslope, riding along the flank of the hill, which was volcanic rock and overgrown with nopal cactus for the most part. Cougar found the position he wanted, a little tongue of projecting, pocked red rock, and there he sat on the buckskin and waited as the rider in the blue uniform guided his horse up the draw. Briefly Cougar lifted his eyes to survey the land, and across the valley he could make out the other trailing soldier. He was a hundred yards or so off, riding in the open, sitting his horse with a rigidity that indicated nervousness to Cougar.

The buckskin shifted its feet and Cougar stroked its neck, calming it as he waited. The man below still had no idea that Carroll Cougar was watching him, that he existed. He had been sent back to look around and that was what he was doing, but he was awkward and unsure in his movements, apparently with little idea of how war was waged on the American continent. His superiors, however, seemed to know — that was why the invading armies had wanted the Apaches, the acknowledged masters of guerilla warfare, on their side.

The uniformed man was near enough now. Still keeping to the brush. Perhaps he felt more secure there, hidden by the clutter of manzanita and willows. Cougar lifted his rifle to his shoulder, and the movement, caught from the corner of his eye, caused the soldier below to react, swinging his own weapon toward Cougar, his eyes wide with surprise. Cougar fired, the big .56 roaring out an echo which drifted far enough across the plains to cause anyone ahead to halt and look back.

Already Cougar was on his second target, the soldier across the valley. He adjusted his sights for windage and distance, sighted on the uniformed man and squeezed off a second shot.

It seemed a minute or so before the bullet tagged him, though it was no longer than half a fatal second. The man threw up his arms and tumbled from his horse, his foot catching in the stirrup so that the panicked mount dragged him bouncing roughly across the rocky ground. The soldier didn't mind a bit: he was already dead, as was the one below Cougar in the ravine. Cougar slowly reloaded, his eyes searching the distances, half-expecting more riders to appear. When none did, he started on, still tracking, following the murderer, who had just lost himself two of his soldiers.

Solon Reineke would ride faster now toward his goal, but it would do him no good, none at all. They didn't make horses fast enough to outrun a bullet, and from now on it was going to be a shoot-and-run war until the last man — Reineke — was the only one left alive.

And then he could face Cougar alone.

2

General George Crook was concerned. He had been behind Fox Ring's main band of warriors for two days and the enemy Apaches continued to run. His aide-de-camp, Major Roger Huggins, studied his commander's worried, weather-lined face and said cheerfully, 'We'll chase them all the way to Mexico at this rate.'

'Why is he running?' Crook said, as if to himself. *Why?* It wasn't Fox Ring's way. The Apache leader was known to them for sharp, deadly forays, for his skilled running battles, but not for fleeing before the blue-jackets.

'We outnumber him greatly,' Huggins said. Crook glanced at the officer but said nothing. Huggins was only newly arrived from the east and hadn't seen the Apaches fight as Crook had.

'No, we're just about even,' Crook answered with a tight smile. Fox Ring didn't need half the numbers that the soldiers had. Crook's troopers were bound together, always mounted as they advanced, almost always dependent on direct commands from their officers to act, while Fox Ring's warriors were free to form into smaller bands, strike and dissipate like smoke in the desert. 'He's drawing us deeper into the mountains,' Crook believed. 'We'll be running low on provisions soon. If his men can live off the land, I'm afraid we can't. We don't have the water we need for our horses. The rain helped some, but traveling in large groups like this, well . . . those little ponds and *tinajas* the Apaches can use don't suit our needs.'

But what was Fox Ring's overall strategy? What was his plan? Where was he leading them and why? 'I don't like this, Roger,' the general said. 'I don't like it a bit. Something is being planned for us.' Something. But *what*?

'All we can do is continue pursuit,' Huggins said unhelpfully.

'Perhaps,' Crook was forced to agree, but he was already thinking along the lines of possible withdrawal on this campaign. He had been considering that for the last two days as Fox Ring continued to fail to engage them. They constantly saw small bands, a man or two, three or more ahead of them along the ridges, among the rocks. This caused Crook's force to slow and approach with still greater caution, but nothing came of these encounters, not even harassing fire. Fox Ring was up to something that Crook could not define.

They couldn't follow the Apache endlessly among these gray, broken hills and twisted canyons where the Apache, when he chose to be, was invisible and the soldiers all-too visible. The army's horses wore down, losing shoes and energy, straining tendons. Crook's soldiers' attention lagged and their provisions faded.

For a little while more he would pursue, Crook decided, lifting his eyes to the jagged high peaks. A half-day, a day. But there was something wrong, something very wrong in the way Fox Ring was behaving, not even trying to inflict occasional casualties on the weary, wandering blue-jackets. And it worried Crook.

It worried him greatly.

If it could be called a smile, Carroll Cougar was smiling. His mouth was twisted, his teeth clamped together. There was no smile in his eyes, however.

One of Reineke's men had been selected to lead the horses out of camp to water at a small, muddy, reed-clotted pond after Reineke's party had made night camp. Dusk was a blur of purple and red-orange, reflected in the water of the pond. The man with the horses looked nervously around, clutching his rifle tightly.

Cougar had been planning some devastation and now he proceeded to carry it out. He was sitting cross-legged on a knoll where a twin oak had split in half and fallen although the leaves were still green and bright.

The butt plate of his Spencer was

cool, pressed tightly to his shoulder as he squeezed off the shot that spun the soldier at the watering hole around. The horses, four of them, took off at a flat-out run across the desert while answering fire from the sheltered camp below was directed at Cougar. Lead spattered into the trunks of the trees and dusted him with bark and earth.

Cougar rolled over the trunk of the tree and moved in a crouch back to where his own horse stood ground hitched, its eyes startled by the gunfire. Mounting, Cougar began to move again, riding in a wide circle, wanting to come up on the far side of the camp where he would wait until morning. Then again he would go about his deadly work, trimming down the ranks of Solon Reineke's little army.

One of the horses, Cougar saw, had stepped on its reins or run itself out and was milling near the camp. It would be caught up before long. There were three men left in Reineke's party including the little popinjay Cougar had seen earlier. Three men and one horse unless they got lucky. In the morning someone would be walking across the desert.

Assuming there were any of them left by morning.

Whistling through his teeth, Cougar tipped back the faded old cavalry hat and guided the buckskin on a miles-long circuit of Reineke's camp.

'You know now for sure, don't you, Solon Reineke?' he said to himself. 'You know for sure that old Cougar's on your trail. Have a good night's sleep, you bastard!'

It was the hour before dawn when Cougar approached the far side of Reineke's camp and he cursed softly at what he found. He had been guilty of underestimating his man. Already the camp was empty. The fire that burned low there was for no one. Reineke had led his people on a night march, leaving Cougar far behind.

No, Cougar thought not for the first time, Reineke hadn't forgotten everything he had been taught. Nor had he forgotten Cougar's ways. Cougar's own horse was weary, needing rest badly. There was nothing to do but swing down, let the horse drink its fill at the muddy pond, and walk the buckskin for a while, slowly trailing Reineke by the light of the fading silver moon.

Cougar had miscalculated his quarry. He did not realize yet that it was not the only mistake he had made that day for he, too, was being followed. He should never have left Fox Ring alive.

★ ★ ★

The Apache leader ran smoothly through the coolness of the predawn hours. He had shed the white man's clothes he had worn for the meeting at Trampas, and now felt free, at one with the desert, his home, his Mother. Fox Ring knew all too well that a man can run a horse down if he was dogged enough. Had he himself not once caught a splendid gray horse that way? It had taken him three days but the animal had wearied while Fox Ring's resolve had not faded.

The man he ran after now rode a weary animal; that was obvious by the strides the horse was now taking, marked clearly in the sand. It was traveling at no more than a walk. Not only was that in Fox Ring's favor, but he knew the land inch by inch. Each ridge and canyon was a place where he had once played — or once warred.

Then, too, he knew where the big man was going even if Cougar himself did not know his destination. Fox Ring would catch him and dispatch him. It had to be done. The big man had to die and that was all there was to it. What Cougar was attempting to do now — for whatever reason — would ruin the grand alliance Fox Ring had joined, an alliance that would return the Apaches to their lands and free them forever from invading American soldiers. *That* had to be effected. Fox Ring would not see his people growing up in slavery as Quiet Star had on that filthy reservation. Their children would live as free as the wind.

Therefore the big man must die before he could reach Crook.

Why, Fox Ring had to wonder, had Cougar chosen to follow Reineke and the field marshal instead of proceeding on his own into the White Mountains? What was their private battle about? It did not matter, the Apache decided. Cougar must die; only that mattered.

Fox Ring loped on across the blue-black night desert sands, scaling dunes and rocky ridges almost effortlessly with his young, strong legs, legs that had run endless miles in play and in earnest. Legs that would surely chase down that horse he was pursuing. And then — no matter that the big man had showed Fox Ring mercy — he would be killed.

If his and Quiet Star's children were to live free, so it must be.

★ ★ ★

Calvin D'Arcy was pinned down. His gray horse was down, lying still as death not ten feet from him. D'Arcy again cursed his crippled arm. If he had not had to use his right for the reins, he could have brought a weapon into action quickly enough to stop the Apache who had popped up from behind the boulders in his path, killing his horse. As it was, D'Arcy had been forced to draw and fire left-handed from the back of his mortally wounded horse, and then the animal had given under him, flopping on to its side as D'Arcy kicked free of the stirrups.

Now he was stuck in a little rocky notch partway up a low hill, not knowing where the Apache had gone, knowing with frustration that he had probably ruined his chances of finding Crook in time to save his life and prevent the triggering of all-out war across the territory.

His hair hung in his eyes, his hat rested near the dead horse just below him. D'Arcy was seated against the rocky bluff behind him, his cocked Colt in his hand, staring at the night. He was waiting. Just waiting. His arm hurt abominably, worse than when it had been shot. He lifted it with his other hand and placed the useless appendage on his lap, trying to lessen the pain, but it was useless.

Damnit, he should be up and moving, but who knew what awaited him out there, how many there were. It was possible that he had been shot by a single warrior he had just happened to encounter. Possible the warrior had gone off or would return with others to search for D'Arcy. Possible that his wild, offhand shot had by sheer luck tagged the Indian mortally.

But it was more likely that there were ten pairs of dark eyes on his position right now, waiting for the white scout to make one fatal error. And so he sat and watched and waited, hoping only that Cougar had been able to find Reineke and eliminate him, thereby removing the threat against Crook from his end of things. One of them must succeed.

The hours passed. D'Arcy could hear the rustling of the twisting wind in the brush around him, whispering nature's primitive songs. A little sand trickled past him from the dark bluff above. He twitched his gun hand at the sound. Nothing. Each small sound was cause for alarm now. Damn all, he didn't want to die out here on this forlorn desert. D'Arcy cursed the day Colonel Plunkett had sought him out and sent him on this mission. He could have been sitting comfortably in that saloon in Nacogdoches, dealing faro while Sarah hung on his shoulder, her scent —

A pebble hit D'Arcy on the hand and he wheeled, looking upward. The Apache had worked his way above him, had he? D'Arcy quietly cocked the Colt and shrunk back, pistol held up, ready to fire.

Then he saw a man's face, but it wasn't an Apache. It was the face of the grinning, one-eyed Dallas McGee! Old

18

friend and now a scout along with him and Cougar for Crook.

What in the hell . . . ?

D'Arcy saw McGee put a finger to his lips and disappear for a moment. Then a rope was tossed down from above and D'Arcy grabbed it like a drowning man grabs a lifeline. He holstered his gun, looked once more below him and then put his boot into the loop at the end of the line.

McGee glanced over again and nodded. D'Arcy waited what seemed to be interminable moments and then was jerked up, bumping and scraping up the bluff until finally he found himself on level ground, seeing McGee dismount from his horse to stride toward him.

'Y'OK?' the Texan, McGee asked, crouching down beside him in the night.

'Where in hell did you come from?' D'Arcy asked. He slipped his boot from the lariat loop and rose shakily to grasp his friend's hand.

'Followed you — all the way from

Fort Apache. I need to find Crook too. After you talked to that man, Pointer, I knew that the captain had pointed out the direction from the worried look on his face.'

'And you, did anyone follow you, Dallas?'

'No. I was real careful about watching my back-trail.'

'Dammit all, Dallas, you weren't supposed to — '

'To what? Save your butt?' McGee asked with a grin.

'Well . . . ' Embarrassed, D'Arcy gave up on his scolding. 'Did you see how many Indians there were?'

'Not for sure. I saw two of them — but even that could've been the same man showing himself twice. But there's no large band of them around.'

'You don't have an extra horse, I don't suppose.'

'No. I didn't figure to need one. We'll have to double up until we find Crook.'

'All right,' D'Arcy said with a long sigh. 'I can't figure out why I haven't found the general already.'

McGee was looking across the canyon to the wide plateau opposite and he raised a pointing finger and said, 'It's no wonder you didn't find him. Look.'

D'Arcy turned and by the thin starlight he could just make out a long line of cavalry riding north, returning to Fort Apache. 'He's going back to the post. Why?' D'Arcy asked in puzzlement.

McGee shrugged. 'No way of knowing. Some sort of change in plans.'

It was frustrating to say the least after all D'Arcy had been through trying to reach the general. The question was now, how did they cut back across the canyon and reach Crook, knowing that there were at least a few Apache warriors prowling around?

'There's a crossing at Brambletree — do you know it? It means continuing south for a little way, putting us further behind, but we can't wait here.'

'No,' McGee agreed. 'We'll try it that

way. Of course there's no guarantee we will make it one piece, Calvin. After all — '

There was not much of a sound to it. Only a little 'thunk' the arrow made as it buried itself in Dallas McGee's chest. The one-eyed man pawed at his holstered six-gun and staggered back. He was still half-grinning in the same old way as his knees buckled and he fell face-first to the ground.

D'Arcy had whirled and dropped to a knee and he saw the bare-chested Apache half-screened by the sagebrush. From his knee he triggered off two rounds from his .44 pistol and saw the Indian spin around, a muffled cry rising from his lips like the howl of a distant coyote suddenly silenced.

Still the Indian came forward and D'Arcy, rising to his feet, shot the warrior again. D'Arcy braced his feet, straddling Dallas McGee's body, and fired again. His third shot caught the onrushing Indian in the neck, his fourth in his head. Then D'Arcy was standing over the fallen Apache and he shot him again as his own chest rose and fell with fury. He kicked the fallen Indian's body and then kicked it again. Then, realizing what he was doing, realizing that he was wasting time, he hurried back to where McGee lay sagged against the yellow earth, blood staining his shirt front, one hand on the shaft of the arrow, the other twitching feebly.

D'Arcy looked up at him blankly. Blood trickled from the corner of his mouth — pinkish, frothy blood rising from a damaged lung.

'Ah, hell, it's nothin',' Calvin D'Arcy told him.

Dallas tried to laugh but choked on his own blood.

'Hell, no. Nothin' . . . '

'We'll just unplug this arrow from you and . . . ' D'Arcy couldn't continue with his too-blatantly false assurances. Lying was no good. What were they going to do? Cut the arrowhead out of Dallas McGee's lung? Rush him to a surgeon when there was nothing that could be done anyway? Pray?

'I'm done,' Dallas said, staring at the cold sky. 'Oh, well, it releases me from my debts, doesn't it?' He tried to grin, but he didn't have the strength even for that. He coughed horribly, his body racked by spasms.

'You'll make it, old son,' D'Arcy said, seating himself beside his friend on the hard earth.

'Sure. Oh, well, D'Arcy. I had a good run.'

'Yeah, that's the only way to look at it,' D'Arcy said, sitting cross-legged beside McGee, watching the life flow out of him.

'Sure.' Then Dallas McGee's hand shot out and with surprising strength he gripped D'Arcy's wrist. His eyes focused sharply. 'You've got to do it, Calvin. For me. You've got to promise.'

'What are you talking about, Dallas?'

'You know what I mean,' the one-eyed scout replied in a weaker voice. 'Do it for me. You tell Cougar how it was with Carlina Polk.'

'Dallas . . . ' D'Arcy fumbled for words.

'For me,' Dallas said again in a near-whisper. 'I'm dying, Calvin. I'm asking for one last favor. I put my life on the line coming out here after you, didn't I?'

'You did.' D'Arcy knew that it could have been, maybe should have been, him lying near death from an Apache arrow. 'But, Dallas, telling Cougar the truth about the woman, I don't know if I can do it.'

'That's all I'm asking. One last favor. You tell Cougar how it was with Carlina.'

'Dallas.'

'Promise me!'

D'Arcy nodded his head weakly. Hell, the odds were he would never see Carroll Cougar again anyway — one or both of them were bound to die out on this wretched desert before this was done. 'I will,' he said.

'I want your word!' Dallas McGee said intently, his eyes searching D'Arcy's.

'My word. I'll tell Cougar how it was.'

Dallas tried to add something, but he didn't even have that much strength. He simply winked his good eye and then he did no more. Dallas was dead and, rising, D'Arcy stood silently in the desert night for a minute, cursing and praying at once. He grabbed Dallas's wallet from inside his vest in case there were addresses of family or friends in it, stripped him of his gunbelt so that no Apache should have it, and then, stepping into the saddle of Dallas McGee's black horse, he jerked its head around and rode out of there at a hard gallop, his eyes on the distant column of smoky dust being raised by General Crook's retreating cavalry.

3

Ellen White had been standing watching sunset color the western sky from the porch in front of the quarters of Captain and Mrs. Rebecca Pointer. The soldiers were standing retreat across the parade ground, assembled near the central flagpole. The sundown skies seemed low and violent above the southern mountains. The fort, home normally to hundreds of troopers, now seemed nearly empty and desolate.

Rebecca Pointer had been watching Ellen, the stranded girl who had been brought to the fort by Carroll Cougar following her father's death on the long desert. Now the older woman stepped out of the door and came up beside her. Rebecca Pointer had sharp planes to her dark face, but her blue eyes were kind. She was even shorter than the girlish Ellen White, compact but lithe.

'It's always a sad time of day for me — retreat,' Rebecca Pointer said.

'Is it?' Ellen responded quietly, almost indifferently.

'Brighten up, dear,' Rebecca said, putting her arm around the younger woman's shoulder. 'Life takes terrible dips at times. It can also take magnificent surges.'

'Yes,' Ellen said somberly. She turned to face Rebecca Pointer, taking her hands. 'I'm going to be of no use at all out here, you know that. And how can I get home with all the trouble out there? There is no way.' There were tears standing in her eyes and Rebecca felt her heart melt with sympathy. As the wife of a career officer she had seen so much, been discouraged so often. This woman was little more than a child. Ellen seemed to believe that her life had ended when in fact it had hardly begun.

'It's not true that you're of no use!' Rebecca protested. 'You help with the sewing and the cleaning. You've been a great companion to me. It's been so long since I've had another woman to talk to. You are helping me — for now let's leave it at that. You're just not yourself again yet. It won't be long until you're able to see things in a different, better light.'

'Yes,' Ellen said, not knowing what she was agreeing to. Thoughts of her father's gruesome death plagued her night and day. She had lost him forever. She had lost Cougar, who had saved her but seemed indifferent to her. She had lost home, church, friends all at once. A sudden new concern lit her eyes. 'We are safe here, in the fort, aren't we?'

'Of course we are,' Rebecca answered soothingly. 'The Apaches would have no chance against us here and they know it. Why ask such a foolish question?'

'I don't know,' Ellen replied, and to be honest she didn't really know why that was a sudden worry. But if a man such as Carroll Cougar had seemed worried about things . . . There was so much going on that she did not know, that no one would tell her!

Ellen asked Rebecca, 'When your husband rides out, when you don't know if he's safe or not for days on end, how do you manage?'

'I manage because I am a warrior's wife and I must manage,' Rebecca said with firm pride.

That was no answer to Ellen at all. She wanted to open up her heart and say how she felt without her warrior, Cougar, how she had somehow grown even closer to him now that he was gone. That she missed his burly, comforting presence; but she said nothing.

Perhaps she was not made to be a warrior's wife.

'Let's start supper, shall we?' Rebecca suggested in the awkward silence and, with a nod, Ellen trailed after her into her quarters, looking only once toward the massive front gates of the post as if by some miracle Cougar would come riding in from out of the sunset at that moment and take her away from all of this fear and uncertainty.

The Apache rode up to them in a storm of dust, his pony badly lathered, and Reineke's mouth tightened. The Indians took no care of their horses. They would ride them to death and then simply steal another. To be honest, Solon Reineke admitted that he hated Indians, all of them. Sometimes it was all he could do to look at them. He hated their smell, their haughty dignity, their ignorance. Now, however, he reined up expectantly, his face expressionless, as the Indian scout reported to him and Field Marshal Von Etzinger.

'Now we are massed and ready,' the Apache said breathlessly, 'but now Crook is returning to the fort.'

Reineke allowed himself a small, humorless smile at the Prussian's discomfort. Von Etzinger tugged at his little waxed mustache and swore.

'Why has he done this? He returns too soon! Fox Ring was required to keep the general in pursuit in the mountains. The man has suspicions. I am concerned! My soldiers are still at the Trampas. We have disorganization!' The field marshal's furious rant failed to impress Solon Reineke.

'Don't worry. We've still got him trapped,' Reineke promised. He was more confident by far than the Prussian. For a time Crook had fallen for the ploy Reineke himself had devised — to follow a few dozen of Fox Ring's warriors aimlessly through the tangle of mountain canyons believing them to be the Apaches' main force while the gathered opposition army slipped into position north of Fort Apache, ready to attack the post at the moment the signal was given that Crook was dead.

No matter — Crook had been misled long enough for Fox Ring's forces to mass before becoming wary of the Apaches' intentions, suspecting a trap, or simply running out of provisions. True, Reineke would have preferred to have had Von Etzinger's force, especially the artillery in position to destroy the fort and all within, but no matter. Reineke was certain that they could hold the fort under siege until the Prussian armaments could be brought up.

The Mexican contingent, under General Diaz, was being held in reserve just this side of the border. They, understandably, were reluctant to enter the fray until there was little doubt left as to the outcome of this adventure. The bitter memory of their defeat and subsequent loss of territory in the Mexican-American War lingered. And, if that was a part of the impetus for their cooperating in this effort, it was nevertheless a motive for extreme caution on their part. They had no wish to see Mexico City assaulted by American cannon again.

Reineke understood that, as he understood the Apaches' desire for revenge and wish to retain their desert lands. He also understood the Prussians' wish to finally establish a foothold on the new continent, having been beaten back in such attempts by the French, the Spanish and later the Americans. Reineke knew and understood each of these elements and he played upon them like an orchestra leader. For himself, he desired nothing less or more than a million square miles of southwestern land with himself as master of the new breakaway republic. It was just beyond their grasp. Just . . . Reineke could nearly taste victory. By the time eastern US army units could be sent west, it would all be over, the land defended by masses of foreign and indigenous forces under Reineke's command.

He told the Apache rider, 'Tell your people that I find this only a minor problem. Assure Fox Ring that within two days Reineke will have done what he has promised and his people may rise up without fear.'

'Tell . . . ?' The Apache looked completely confused. 'Where is Fox Ring? He was to be with you. Did he not meet with you at the Trampas?'

'He is coming,' Reineke lied, having no idea where in hell the Apache renegade leader was at the moment or why he had failed to join up with them. 'Soon Fox Ring will be here to take command. For now, reassure your people and tell them to begin massing for the attacks.'

The Indian was obviously suspicious, Reineke saw. He was probably wondering if the duplicitous whites had taken Fox Ring prisoner, maybe even killed him. Reineke saw all that pass behind the Apache's eyes, smiled a treacherously reassuring smile and rested his hand on the messenger's shoulder although he would as soon have shot him. When this was done, Reineke considered, the Apaches would find themselves in a worse situation than they were enduring now. The messenger rode away slowly, looking back over his shoulder mistrustfully. Then he lifted his exhausted pony into a more rapid gait and vanished into the desert distances.

'Where is Fox Ring?' Von Etzinger asked with apparent concern.

'Dead. I didn't see the body, but he was tracking Cougar. If Cougar is alive, Fox Ring is dead. I assure you of that,' Reineke said.

'You are sure?' the Prussian asked, studying Reineke's eyes. 'So, it is done!'

'It is done.' They could have used Fox Ring as an ally, but Reineke figured he could still manage the Apaches. They would fight once they saw the Europeans draw first blood and saw a chance for recovering their lands by joining the battle, with or without Fox Ring at their head. There was still that outspoken woman — what was her name? Quiet Star? Fox Ring's wife — to be controlled, but she too could be managed. Reineke thought he would allow her to take charge if it came to that, assuming she had such power. Why not? It would have been easier with the more fanatical Fox Ring, but if the man was dead, well then. He was dead.

But Fox Ring was not dead. Even now he was within striking distance of the big man on the buckskin horse who trailed Reineke's party. Why did he delay attacking the big man? The white was his enemy; and yet he had spared Fox Ring's life. It puzzled Fox Ring, and he was a man who disliked uncertainty.

Deciding, the Apache leader shook his head. There was no point in thinking about it. What did it matter in the end what the big man had done, who he was or why he had done what he did? The man would die. He must die.

And Fox Ring would be the one to kill him.

★ ★ ★

Cougar had pulled his bandana up over his face. The wind had risen and blow sand was sifting over him. Still the faithful buckskin horse plodded on. Cougar had picked up Reineke's trail an hour after dawn. Now it was dusk and he had the slow-moving party in his sights once more.

A rider — an Apache, he had thought from that distance — had ridden in, spoken briefly to Reineke and then ridden out again. Cougar could only speculate on the substance of that conversation. It indicated that there were more Apaches in the area, however. Cougar wondered if D'Arcy had yet managed to reach Crook. If so, the instant Reineke showed his face, he would be arrested by army authorities.

Cougar shifted in his saddle to look behind him, a customary cautious habit of his, but he could see little through the blow sand, which was deepening and darkening as the sun began its descent. He urged his horse on, trying to stay close to Reineke before he could lose himself in the obscuring sand. He could not risk losing the man now.

Dusk settled moodily through the sandstorm. Shadows appeared, pooled and disappeared in a mysterious, tangled array, changing shape and speed. Cougar began to wonder if this was going to build to a full-blown sandstorm, the sort that hides all, disguises all and makes travel itself impossible, where the only concern was to protect eyes and try to keep from smothering.

There seemed no doubt now that Reineke, instead of entering the White Mountain foothills, intended to ride to Fort Apache, and Cougar found that confusing. He knew only that Reineke meant to — must, if his plan were to succeed — kill General Crook and raise the insurrection. How Reineke intended to carry out the assassination, Cougar could not guess, but he had to stop Solon Reineke.

If he failed in that the entire southwest was going to go up in a firestorm. Even if Reineke's grandiose scheme failed and his army was beaten back, it was going to cost many men their lives. Thousands, perhaps. Unconsciously Cougar urged his horse on even faster, although the big horse's strength was obviously on the wane; it staggered now and then in its exhaustion and thirst.

The sandstorm, if it continued, Cougar thought, would give him excellent cover for moving in on Reineke. Now he had given up the idea of facing the man down in single combat and eliminating him. That concept, he realized, had been selfish. The larger good, stopping the coming war, was more important than personal vengeance. Reineke had to be taken down and it did not matter how it was done. Not when Cougar considered the results if he failed in his mission — the burned-out houses and stripped fields, the crying of children, the wailing of women, the blood of the warriors from both sides staining the sands of the desert to crimson.

Cougar's head lifted suddenly with the crack of the shot near at hand. There was an instant of surprise, then one of shocked awareness. Then the stunning pain and realization. He had been shot from cover.

The bullet had ripped through his thigh and thudded into the body of his horse, and now the buckskin was falling as Cougar kicked free of the stirrups and threw himself away from the stumbling animal.

A second shot, fired as he fell, narrowly missed killing him, ripping a furrow across the back of his skull as he slammed clumsily to the ground.

He was free of the horse, dazed but conscious. Instinctively he rolled behind the still-quivering buckskin as three more shots pounded against the unfortunate animal's body.

And then the big horse was still and the desert silent except for the keening of the wind. Sand obliterated all in the dusky hour. Cougar shook his head, trying to clear it, but it felt as if someone had sledgehammered his skull. He tried to focus his eyes, to think, but nothing was clear. Sand swirled past in funnels and curtains, like a dry storm washing over him. The body of the dead buckskin was heated. There was a fiery pain in his thigh as if someone had torn a hole through muscle and fiber with a red-hot poker.

Where was his rifle? He searched the hot sand for the familiar heft of the Spencer .56. It was gone, lost in the sand and the darkness. It took him a long minute to realize that he still had his Winchester needle gun in the saddle scabbard. He groped for the .44–40, but found it trapped beneath the tremendous weight of the buckskin. Cougar yanked furiously at it, each tug bringing excruciating pain to thigh and skull, but it finally came free in his hands. Yet he had no target under the prevailing conditions and — had he one — he doubted that he was capable of hitting it no matter how near.

Move, dammit! a distant voice insisted, and groggily Cougar did just that, drawing himself to his feet with the assistance of the rifle stock as pain flared ferociously in his thigh. Hobbling, he made a staggering run toward a mesquite-and nopal-filled hollow fifty feet away. Two shots from the heart of the dark, sandy confusion dogged his tracks, both missing badly, both fired from an invisible source.

Cougar flopped more than dove into the sheltered hollow, and as he landed pain tore through his skull. It felt as if little men were now attempting to pry the top of it off. The pain in his thigh faded into insignificance although Cougar knew it was the far more dangerous wound. He could feel his trouser leg growing heavy, sopped with an unstoppable flow of blood.

Cougar blinked his sand-filled eyes and then rubbed them hard, increasing the abrading. His vision was blurred badly and he could not clear it. Something moved, or perhaps it was only one of those constantly shifting shadows through the sand. He thought he saw a man darting toward him on the right. Levering a round into the Winchester's receiver, he tried to sight down on the shadowy figure, but then the man — if it was truly a man — was gone again, vanished in the swirling, dusk-darkened sandstorm.

Cougar wanted to move again, not caring for his position with the possibility that he had been spotted, but he wasn't sure if he had the strength to move. Nor did he want to rise up without knowing who was watching, what they had seen.

Silence again. Only the hiss of the shifting sand. It grew darker yet. That made his mind up for him. He could move with near-impunity as darkness settled and the sandstorm's fury increased. If his last movement had been detected, his enemy knew where he was and had only to wait for his chance.

★   ★   ★

Maybe it was best to just hunker down. Maybe he would run right into their arms if he moved. Cougar was briefly lost in confusion as his head rang and spun. He forced his mind to clear, to *think*.

Move, damn you, Cougar! Turning carefully in the little hollow, carrying his Winchester cocked, he started to climb out of the depression through the cactus and mesquite and then clamber up the hill behind it.

There was only the sweat in his eyes, the flow of warm blood down his pant-leg and the back of his neck, the darkness of the settling night, the obscurity of the devilish sandstorm. He found himself on his belly and realized he had passed out from lack of blood.

Forcing himself to rise, Cougar moved up the hill which was black, porous volcanic stone strewn across the earth and much cholla cactus. He fell into a patch of these 'jumping cacti' and came up studded with their painfully imbedded segments.

He now realized that his Winchester, too, was gone, lost in the turmoil of the night.

There was nothing he could do about that. He continued to climb, falling more times than he could count, light-headed and feeling as if he had misplaced his very skeleton. His hands were torn by rocks as sharp as razors, his knees bruised and ripped.

He crawled and stumbled and fell through a nightmare. He could see nothing at all as night became fully dark. Still the sand blew, howling around him, stinging eyes and clogging ears and nostrils.

How far had he climbed? How much further *could* he climb? Now his head simply buzzed and ached like a roaring hangover; the wounded leg had taken precedence. With each step it threatened to buckle. It was stiff and rubbery at once. Blood filled Cougar's boot. He labored his panting way on, moving upward, seeking safety in the heights as a mountain lion does when wounded.

The sandstorm seemed to lessen as he went higher, but the darkness seemed more total. He had a fear now of stepping into some unseen chasm and falling to his death. He had more fear of the weapons behind him. He crept on — the cougar climbing toward safety. Was his enemy still at his heels, hunting stealthily, confidently? There was no way of knowing. Without thought now Cougar climbed and fell and clawed his way upward.

Abruptly he fell again. This time his tumble dropped him fifteen feet or so to land against solid earth, forcing the breath from his lungs with the impact. He sat up sharply with a stifled groan. He felt around him cautiously, finding nothing of use. The ground beneath him was gravelly. That was all he knew and all he was to know for a long time as the pain and deprivation rose up and rolled over him, driving him down into deep unconsciousness . . .

★ ★ ★

Something clawed uncomfortably at Cougar's eyes and he made the ultimate effort of lifting his eyelids. He closed them again immediately, for yellow-white daylight seared his eyes as he looked upward from where he had fallen. Turning his head slightly he tried opening them again, squinting cautiously at his surroundings. He was looking up a shaft of stone, he discovered, some sort of natural chimney into which he had fallen the night before. He lay now in a sinkhole some thirty feet deep, in a hollow washed out by eons of rain and perhaps at one time from underground springs flowing there.

Cougar looked around slowly. The trapped position where he lay was lost in deep shadow except for the high, direct sun overhead. He couldn't estimate the size of the crevice. Not far from him lay the skeleton of a desert sheep — another victim of the hidden sinkhole.

Cougar tried to rise, and immediately sat again as the banging in his skull increased and his leg screamed with pain. He lay back again and stared at the light above him. Just stared, unable to gather the strength to attempt movement.

Without realizing it, he slept — or rather passed out — again. When he awoke it was still light, but he couldn't have said if it was a new day or a week of days since he had fallen. But it was light at least. He did not fear the darkness, but to spend another night in that barren hole was intolerable.

He raised himself slowly to a sitting position, his arms trembling with weakness. He patted his hip hopefully — yes, the Colt was still there, thank God. Though what good it was ever going to do him he couldn't have said. Cougar was shivering now although he knew that it was warm enough so that he shouldn't be. Shakily he drew his bowie and slit open his pantleg. The wound in his thigh was clean enough, the bullet having passed all the way through it, boring a neat hole, yet it had bled much and would continue to bleed if something weren't done, and his body was manufacturing no new blood just then without food or water. He surveyed the wound with his shaggy head hanging miserably. There was little he could do. He had nothing to work with. He cut a long strip of cloth from the tail of his shirt and wrapped it around the bullet-hole area so tightly that it hurt, knotting it down deliberately, clenching his teeth as he did so.

That done, he fingered the back of his scalp, finding a bloody mat of hair and beneath it the furrow grooved there by the ambusher's bullet. There was little he could do to treat that either. Again he tore a long strip of cloth from his shirt and bound it tightly around his skull. The effort of these two tasks exhausted him and he lay back panting, pain pulsing through his body from toes to skull.

The sky was now growing dark above him, the chimney in nearly complete shadow. It had to be done! He forced himself to rise in excruciating pain and survey the shaft overhead. Three feet wide or so, only, it was formed of basaltic rock. The blue sky seemed impossibly distant. He rested a hand on the wall of the chimney and shook his head at the impossibility of climbing out in his present condition. Again, from the corner of his eye, he caught sight of the skeleton of the dead sheep. Soon, perhaps, his bones would be lying beside it. He beat his helpless hand against the stone wall. A bitter curse filled his mouth and was bellowed out to echo through the cavern. It was over. He was done.

Reineke had won the battle.

4

The dead man rose.

So it seemed to Carroll Cougar. He had somehow gotten to his feet again. His leg was trembling violently. At one point he had again fallen unconscious. Now, emerging from that coma-like state, fresh pain flooded over him and bitter frustration. But a new emotion was shoving both aside. This was a strong emotion indeed that he now felt — pure, dark hatred. Hatred of Solon Reineke and a terrible anger that the bastard might get away with what he had done, let alone what he was now planning to do, while Cougar sat alive yet impotent in this tomb nature had carved for him.

Surging anger drew him to his feet, and he searched the cavern for anything that might be of use. There was just nothing — nothing but the rocks that had fallen from the narrow chimney when it was formed.

But if the rocks had fallen, could they not also be put back up? Excitement building, Cougar considered this idea. If a cairn could be built high enough to allow him to reach the chimney proper . . . He got to work.

It was excruciating labor for a man in his condition. First he rolled three huge boulders together and then lifted a flat stone on top of them. He collected a good many head-sized stones and stacked them on this platform as best he could. Long intervals of rest were necessary between each task and by the time he was finished with all that it seemed possible to do, his head was swimming with exhaustion and the sky seen through the mouth of the tunnel was dark and starry.

And yet his labors had only begun.

The next step, if it was possible at all in his present condition, would be debilitating. Cougar rested again for half an hour and then determined to make his try.

Climbing carefully on top of the cairn he had built, he straightened up to find himself nearly into the chimney. He hesitated only briefly. He would never know if he could make it until he tried, and another day in the cavern would see him without the strength to even make the attempt.

With his arms held behind him, his hands on the stone wall of the chute, he lifted his good leg and planted it on the opposite side of the three-foot-by-three-foot chimney. Then, with all the strength he could muster, he lifted his aching body, propping himself between the vertical walls of the chimney until, spiderlike, he began inching his way up in that fashion.

The agony was profound. His head hammered, his leg was torn by pain. Sweat rained from his forehead, stinging his eyes. He could only grit his teeth and inch his way upward, knowing that if he lost his position he would fall again and likely break his back.

The stars above seemed no nearer as

he crabbed his way up the dark chimney, moving first his good leg and then his hands up a few painful inches at a time.

When he was finally up and out, rolled on to flat ground, it was with such relief that a sob rose from the throat of the powerful man. He lay there, quivering and exhausted against the warm earth, beneath the cool, starry sky, feeling that he ought to kiss the sand beneath his face in gratitude. He was still alive.

Yet he had gained almost nothing.

Wounded, afoot, surrounded by the enemy, he was miles from the fort. The success of this mission had to be on D'Arcy. If D'Arcy failed then the game was up. Knowing he would be lucky to make it a hundred yards, Cougar nevertheless got to his feet and shuffled ahead. Finding a dead manzanita tree, he cut a twisted branch from it to use as a cane. He hobbled on doggedly, knowing that he was beaten. He would die out on this lonesome desert.

Struggling for breath, he paused for a bare moment atop the dark hill where he could stare out across mile after empty mile and see not the faintest glimmer of light. Half conscious, he spoke aloud:

'I'm sorry, Ellen. Sorry, girl.' Then he shook his head, lifted his eyes to the stars to take his direction and shambled off across the broken, cactus-strewn, savage land.

★   ★   ★

Calvin D'Arcy was no better off than he had been before Dallas McGee's daring rescue. Not wanting to cross the canyon where he knew there were Apaches, D'Arcy had circled wide of the gorge toward the fort. Approaching from the south on his weary mount, he had nearly ridden into the Indian camp.

D'Arcy's eyes widened in the darkness and he backed his horse carefully until he was half-hidden in the shadows of a group of shaggy cottonwood trees.

He was looking smack down into the largest encampment of Apaches he had ever seen. There were too many to count, spread out across the long, snaking valley, blocking the very route he had intended to follow to the fort.

It was no secret to D'Arcy why they were massed there, but just what could he do about it? The answer was, unfortunately, nothing. He knew he couldn't break through their lines unseen and reach Fort Apache with a warning. All of his long ride had been for nothing.

He would have to backtrack along the very same route he had followed northward, and that would put him hours behind Crook, assuming that he even made it to the fort alive.

D'Arcy cursed slowly and lifted his good arm to wipe his brow where nervous perspiration had sprung out. The wind which had seemed warm now cut coldly to the bone. Most carefully, he backed the black horse even further until he was well hidden from the camp by the cottonwoods. He tried again to come up with a plan for slipping past the nest of Apaches, but nothing sensible came to mind. Slowly then, with many silent curses, he turned his horse back along the trail.

It was all up to Cougar now, D'Arcy thought. He was the only hope they had of warning General Crook and heading off this war. If anyone could do it, it was the big man — that was the only thought D'Arcy had to comfort him as he slipped away into the night of the vast desert and began working his way southward once more.

★ ★ ★

Cougar tripped over an unseen rock, fell and banged his head on another stone. He lay there on the side of the hill, his breath coming in heaving gasps. Fever coursed through his body now. His untreated wounds had grown infected. He could feel the heat beneath the accompanying pain. He couldn't get up again. Dammit! He just couldn't.

Life, after all, was only a game, wasn't it? Very well. He'd overplayed his hand and lost. He wondered vaguely how far he had managed to stumble toward the fort on that night. How much further there was to travel. Too far, he knew, just too damned far. All right, Solon Reineke had won the last hand, won the game. He would have his war, which he seemed to want so badly.

How long he lay there as the stars shifted overhead he did not know, but finally, even knowing that all of his effort was useless, he came to his knees, and with a groan again hoisted himself to his feet where he stood wobbling for a long minute before he started on again.

One step at a time, Cougar, he told himself. One step at a time, although that would not be enough to help Crook. He wanted to get somewhere — anywhere — and not die out on this trackless desert to be devoured by critters, his bones strewn across the sands to bleach.

He felt like a man wading through hip-deep water. Each movement was enormously slow. Someone had strapped anvils to his feet. His head still ached, but he had long ago quit paying attention to that. His leg had overshadowed that pain with its torrents of agony.

'They'll prob'ly have to saw it off,' he muttered to himself. He realized that he had been talking to himself for a long while. Then he laughed in a cracked voice. '*Who'll* saw it off, you idiot? Some Apache?' Because he knew that if he ever lived long enough to see another living human being it would likely be an Apache, and Cougar would be easy pickings indeed. 'Prob'ly be ashamed to take my scalp,' he said. Not much glory in that, was there? Scalping a dead man. Then he laughed again. The laughter worried him. 'Must be losing my mind.'

Cougar shook his head so violently that it brought a new surge of pain to his battered skull, trying to shake it clear. His thinking was fuzzy, not just at the edges, but all the way through. He looked again to his marker stars, making sure that he wasn't walking in circles. No, the Dipper assured him that *that* at least was all right. He was disoriented but not lost. That was something.

He slogged on. There was a light in the sky that puzzled him with its glow. Maybe they had set fire to the fort! No, that was the wrong direction for Fort Apache. What in hell was it, then? And then he realized that he was watching the birth of desert dawn. He had walked through the night and was still alive. Would he be alive to see another dawn?

The sky began to mist with pale color, and doves took to wing, heading for their secret watering places. He saw a coyote scurrying for home. He walked on, his shadow long and crooked in the morning light. He made his way staggering toward tortuous death, stumbling toward its embrace, needing to live.

Cougar realized then that he was no

longer enduring for Crook's sake, nor to stop the war, nor even for his long-sought vengeance on Solon Reineke. He was walking through this earthly hell for Ellen White, to see her face again, to live for her. Only for Ellen.

Methodically, leaning heavily on his cane, he walked on and the day grew hot and the land even more desolate in the brilliant light of day. His throat was parched and constricted, his belly tight with the need for water. And there would be no water.

His lips were cracked and blistered, bleeding. His eyes felt as heavy as lead weights hanging from a gaunt skull. The sun was a branding iron on his neck and back. He wanted to find shade, even the smallest patch of it, but the barren land was devoid even of grease-wood and mesquite. He pushed that thought too from his mind. He would keep moving. No matter how many times he fell, he would walk on, or even crawl, until he reached her.

He waded on through the sands beneath

the searing sun, a small, hobbled dot of a man on the vast spread of the scorched desert. But he was walking. He was alive.

They had not killed the cougar yet.

* * *

Ellen White was scrubbing the wooden kitchen floor with lye soap and a stiff brush when Rebecca Pointer came into the quarters and called out cheerfully, 'Ellen, where are you, dear?'

'Out here. In the kitchen.' Ellen tossed her scrub brush back into the bucket of soapy water and rose, holding the base of her back with one hand.

Rebecca came through the doorway and Ellen asked her, 'How's the floor look?'

'Oh, don't bother about that right now, Ellen. I've got marvelous news!'

Ellen felt her heart leap. Could it be . . . But Rebecca burst that frail bubble of hope before it had fully formed.

'We're going to have a ball! Really,

Ellen. A very important dignitary has arrived at Fort Apache and we're going to welcome him with a dress ball.'

'Oh,' Ellen replied with a limp sigh.

'Cheer up, dear. It'll be good for your spirits, you know. This man has come all the way from Prussia, can you believe that! He's a very high-ranking officer. Not delightful to look at, but charming enough. I spoke to him briefly. So, come with me, let's see if I have anything we can alter for you to wear. There's no time to get new cloth and sew you something, I'm afraid.'

'I really don't think I'd be much fun, Rebecca. Maybe it's best if you forget about me going.'

'With the paucity of ladies we have on this post? The young officers wouldn't forgive me if you didn't come along.'

'I'm really not very interested in young officers, either,' Ellen said, leaning against the kitchen table.

'You'll change your mind. I'll see to it,' Rebecca said encouragingly. 'Meanwhile, you'll certainly help us decorate the hall with bunting, won't you?'

'Of course,' Ellen agreed feebly.

'Good.' Rebecca Pointer smiled in return, putting a motherly arm around her. 'You'll see — decorating will help get you in the mood. And I insist that you at least look at the blue organdy dress I have folded away. You'd look so charming in it, and you must be dying to get into something a little fancier than my old calico housedress.'

'Yes,' Ellen answered, although she couldn't have cared much less about the way she dressed these days.

'At least think about it — going to the ball — won't you, Ellen?'

'I'll at least think about it,' Ellen was forced to answer in the face of Rebecca Pointer's merriment.

But she didn't *care* about a foreign dignitary, and she didn't *care* about the young officers or the ball. All she cared about these days was her big, roughly gentle man who was out there on the desert doing who-knew-what, undoubtedly something quite dangerous. She wished that Cougar had at least told her what it was that demanded his attention.

While Rebecca Pointer went to her clothes trunk, Ellen, wiping her hands on her cleaning dress, went to the doorway of the lieutenant's quarters. With General Crook's return from the field, the parade ground was filled with men going about their business or simply relaxing if they were off duty. It was almost a regular town out there with the homecoming troops drinking beer in front of the sutler's store, with the blanket Indians crouched in the shade along the palisade, speaking in low tones to each other, with the covered wagons of the evacuating settlers and their shouting children cluttering the open areas while a handful of soldiers did punishment drills on the far side of the yard near the stables.

It was almost a regular town these days. A big, crowded, empty town.

Empty. Yes, that was what it was, this teeming fort.

Cougar could have filled the whole place with his broad shoulders and almost bashful grin, with his long-striding frame swaggering through the mob. Without him it was only empty. How long would it remain so? Rebecca called out to her and Ellen turned back toward the interior of the house.

'Here it is, dear,' Rebecca said to Ellen, holding up the dark-blue organdy dress in front of her, turning in a circle. 'You'll look lovely in it. You must try it on for me and let me see how it fits.'

Her voice went on and Ellen tried to admire the dress and smile from time to time at her excitement. But it was no good. All right, then, to make Rebecca happy, she would attend the ball honoring this Prussian, but it would be no good. The hall might be hung with bunting and Chinese lanterns, but none of that would be any good.

It would still be empty, very empty.

5

There was blood all over the mule's pack and on the mule itself. It was wide-eyed with fear, skittish and ready to flee. Yet it stood in the deerfly-infested, airless sandy draw, staring at Cougar, its ears twitching, its hide rippling with excitement as the man approached.

'Stand easy,' Cougar said softly. 'Stand easy, big boy.'

The mule's muscles bunched as if it were ready to leap into a run, but perhaps it had the need to be with a man, for it awaited Cougar's approach, however warily. Cougar could see the two broken arrow shafts in its gray hip. The pack on the animal's back was sideways, but on it hung a canteen.

Cougar had first carefully approached the mule over an hour before, but that time it had run off in panic. Cursing then, Cougar had painfully tracked it to this airless, fly-thick draw.

He had not been able to find the body of the mule's owner. Not that he would have been able to do anything about burying him decently anyway, not in his present state. Now Cougar's eyes were fixed only on the mule. On the mule and that canteen. Life-giving, lovely canteen.

'Easy now. Stand easy, big boy. You're hurtin', aren't you?' His fingertips touched the quivering animal's neck and then his hand snatched the mule's bridle. The mule backed away at that sudden movement, but Cougar kept his grip and after another few minutes had the animal calmed some.

The canteen first!

He untied it from the pack with one hand, drew the cork with his teeth and spat it out and then drank deeply, the revitalizing liquid trickling down his throat into his parched body. He drank again and again. Wanting still more, he instead reached down, retrieved the cork and replaced it.

'Now then,' Cougar said. He didn't bother unfastening the cinches. His bowie knife cut the pack free, and though the mule was still frightened, it seemed happy to be relieved of its burden.

Still holding the mule's reins tightly, Cougar crouched to slash open the pack. There was nothing in it that he had any use for: a pickax, two dirty shirts, a set of scales, a small bag which might or might not have contained gold dust. Cougar didn't bother to find out. Gold was not what he needed.

The mule eyed him warily again as Cougar stood, perhaps having a premonition of what was to come.

'That's right, you long-eared rascal, I'm going to climb aboard.'

He and the mule had entirely different ideas about that. Perhaps it hadn't been ridden for a long time. Perhaps it had never been ridden. It shied and bucked and reared up, but Cougar stayed aboard, clinging to its back. There was no hope at all of cutting the arrowheads out, and if the mule had expected this man-thing to relieve its pain it was no doubt angry and disappointed.

'Too bad. You're stuck with me.'

And with a lot of heeling at the mule, he managed to get it into motion and guide it, stumbling, up and out of the sandy wash, turning its head toward Fort Apache.

The mule plodded across the hot, uninhabited land, its heavy gait bringing pain to Cougar's damaged thigh with each footfall. Still, it beat walking and falling down by a long shot. Cougar allowed himself to drink a little more water and felt much better for it as the liquid found its way to his parched cells. Still, Cougar's sunburned, blistered face was grim with pain and determination and his head pounded in rhythm to the mule's gait.

He still had grave doubts about making it to the fort. He knew full well how weak he was, and the mule was not in much better condition. It hobbled along, its wounded flank undoubtedly spreading infection through its sturdy body. Also Cougar did not believe for a moment that he was alone on the seemingly empty desert. There were many hunters out there. Many watchers.

If he did reach the fort could he possibly make it in time to stop Solon Reineke? That seemed unlikely as well. If he were in time, what kind of struggle could he hope to put up in his current shape? Cougar tried to expel the negative thoughts from his mind, but it wasn't easily done.

Sometimes, too, he rode through a haze his mind had created. The colors of the desert flared up and vanished to return as a vastly distant spectrum of no real substance, a mirage of dreams. The mule seemed to float through strange, swirling mists and Cougar more than once found himself slumped across the animal's neck, clinging to it only out of instinct.

He forced himself to try to clear his

vision, to peer through the weird sky and locate the fort, but there was only him and his stumbling mule in all of the world . . .

Until the man with the rifle in his hands burst up out of the gully and shouted at Cougar.

'Just hold up, right there!'

Cougar automatically reined in the mule, which stood there trembling from exhaustion and illness, its body lathered. Cougar had reached for his holstered Colt, but he could not find it through the mental haze. He was dead if this man meant him harm.

The mist slowly parted and the face of the intruder coalesced into meaningful features as the rider neared him. When it did Cougar could have cried out for joy.

'D'Arcy . . . '

'Cougar?' D'Arcy narrowed his eyes. His mouth turned down in stunned disbelief. 'Jesus, Cougar!' he said, and then the big man felt an arm helping him down from the mule's back. 'Have you any idea what you look like?'

'I've a fair idea, D'Arcy,' Cougar said grimly. His voice was like sandpaper on rough wood.

'No, you don't,' D'Arcy said with a shake of his head. 'You'd have to be on the outside.'

Cougar's pantleg was in shreds. He wore only half a shirt — there was a dirty strip of it wrapped around his head which was matted and clotted with blood. His whiskered face was dirty and battered, his mouth blistered and bleeding, his hands scabbed. Hundreds of festering cactus spine punctures dotted his arms and face, chest and legs. Around his eyes his face was swollen from numerous deerfly bites. His chin, where he had fallen, was split open jaggedly.

'Damn, Carroll, what have you been through?' D'Arcy asked, and he lifted the canteen to Cougar's lips.

'A small section of hell, I guess.'

'Did you get him? Did you get Solon Reineke?' D'Arcy couldn't help asking.

'No.'

'Damn!' D'Arcy swore bitterly.

'Then you weren't able to catch up with Crook?'

'No. He's returned to the fort, though.'

'Then Reineke will be there too, sooner or later,' Cougar said, wiping a filthy, bruised hand across his mouth. 'You'd better ride on ahead, Calvin, and hard.'

'Not without you, Cougar,' Calvin D'Arcy said firmly.

'The mule,' he said, looking at the pitiful beast, 'can't go on any further.'

'Then we'll ride double on my mount. The fort's not more than ten miles.'

'Still too far, with the horse carrying double. You've got to get there.'

D'Arcy was firm. 'I said not without you. Let me have a look at your leg.' He reached for the filthy bandage around Cougar's thigh, but the big man slapped his hands away.

'No, damnit, D'Arcy! There's no time

for any of that now. I'll ride with you if you say so, but damnit, let's get going.'

D'Arcy only nodded his 'OK'. Cougar was right. There was no time at all to lose. Reineke was probably already at the fort, and if he was there, General Crook's time was limited. And when Crook was assassinated, all of the territory was going to explode into violence.

'We're a fine pair,' D'Arcy said with a collapsed smile. 'I can't even help you up behind me, Cougar. It's a hell of a thing living with one arm.'

Calvin D'Arcy struggled into the saddle himself and added, 'But it beats dying with both arms, I guess. Cougar, Dallas McGee is gone. The Apaches got him.'

Cougar nodded, but he only said, 'Let's not let them get us.' And with much effort he clambered up behind D'Arcy and clung to him as the weary black horse was heeled into motion, pounding off toward Fort Apache.

Ellen White looked splendid in her borrowed blue organdy gown which, taken in a little here and let out some there, fitted her perfectly. Her dark hair was piled prettily on top of her head and Rebecca had loaned her a string of pearls which now decorated her long, sleek throat. Captain Pointer had put on his dress uniform and Rebecca Pointer wore a dark-orange dress. Pointer emerged from his bedroom to survey both ladies in their finery.

'Well,' he exclaimed, 'I'll be envied tonight, walking in with you two beauties on my arms.'

Ellen smiled only slightly. She still had ill feelings about this. It seemed almost like a betrayal of Carroll Cougar to be going to a fancy-dress ball while he was out on that trackless desert alone. He would have laughed off her concerns, but she could not, would not.

'Are we ready, then?' Pointer asked, and with one of the ladies on each arm, he led the way toward the hall where the post band was warming up and the varicolored Chinese lanterns shone through the windows and on to the parade ground.

'Who was that hard-looking man that we saw with Field Marshal Von Etzinger?' Rebecca asked her husband as they approached the assembly hall.

'Didn't you recognize him? Perhaps you hadn't come out to join me yet when he was here. Solon Reineke is his name. He used to scout for us. The State Department has hired him to guide Von Etzinger along his western route. Reineke and General Crook were having a grand time reminiscing over brandy.'

'You know,' Elizabeth said, 'I think I do remember him now. It's just that he looks so different in that suit with his hair slicked back. I was used to seeing him in buckskins.'

'Yes,' Pointer said with a laugh, 'Reineke's quite the dude these days, it seems. We did have a good group of scouts when he was here, but Lord! Were they a sight to see when they would come back from reconnaissance in the desert. Of course, when you consider being a week on the desert, half the time crawling on their bellies, nothing to wash with, it was no wonder.'

'There were four of them, weren't there?' Rebecca asked her husband.

'Five, actually. There was Deerfoot, then Reineke, McGee, D'Arcy and of course Cougar!' Pointer said with a laugh.

Ellen's head came up with sudden attention to what the officer was saying. 'Cougar?' she asked hoarsely.

'Yes, and he was the roughest of that lot! What a hell raising man. But even the general admitted that Cougar was the best of them all, undisciplined as he was. There was no one like him for tracking, not even Deerfoot.' Pointer caught Ellen's eyes studying him with a touch of doubt, a hint of sadness. He caught himself.

'Oh, Miss White! I'd forgotten you've met Cougar, haven't you? D'Arcy told me that when he brought you in. I hope I haven't put my foot in it. Is Cougar a friend of yours?'

'Not exactly,' Ellen answered. 'You said nothing to offend me, Lieutenant Pointer.' But she did wonder about the description Pointer had given. Cougar as a wild hell raiser? She had never seen a more somber man. But then, she supposed, many men who were wild in their younger days changed their ways completely as the years passed.

'D'Arcy still hasn't returned, has he?' Rebecca asked.

'No,' Pointer said, shaking his head worriedly. 'We figure that he must have just missed making a connection with the general since Crook had retreated from bivouac and decided to return to post before he had reached Cottonwood Creek. If D'Arcy had taken another, more direct route there, he must have reached that point when the general was already on his way back.

'Or so we hope,' Pointer added in a more subdued voice. D'Arcy and his mission remained a mystery to the lieutenant. If only D'Arcy had confided in him, things might be clearer, but D'Arcy had chosen not to. Or was unable to. Those were his orders, it seemed, and Pointer understood that, but . . .

The door to the assembly hall was opened by an enlisted man, and the three entered the well-lit room, seeing General Crook himself in earnest conversation with Solon Reineke and Field Marshal Von Etzinger. Crook raised his wine glass across the room in a toast to the ladies, and Pointer half-saluted in return.

'The punchbowl, ladies?' Lt. Pointer said, and they walked that way, Ellen drawing admiring gazes from all sides as the young officers became aware of her presence and beauty. Ellen was aware of their stares, but heedless of them. She accepted her glass of pink punch and sipped at it as the band struck up its first number. She took only three small sips and replaced the glass on the table, feeling somehow guilty about enjoying it. Drinking pink lemonade while Cougar . . .

Then a young blond lieutenant bowed to her and introduced himself and she was dancing with him around the polished floor of the hall, hearing his voice without listening to a word he said.

Where are you, Cougar?

★   ★   ★

'There it is!' D'Arcy shouted. 'We're almost there, old-timer.'

Cougar opened his encrusted eyes and pawed at them heavily. Far in the distance, Fort Apache could be dimly seen against the desert floor, and Cougar felt fresh vigor rush through him. They would make it. He would see Ellen again before he died.

The black horse, near total exhaustion, stumbled on toward the dark form of the fort, carrying the two battered scouts. 'Am I going crazy?' Cougar asked D'Arcy through cracked lips. 'I could swear I hear music.'

'If you are going crazy, I am too. I hear it. What in the hell could it be about? It's a weird time for a ball with Fox Ring encircling the post! This is not like Crook at all.'

'He doesn't know Fox Ring's back to the south.'

'No, but still, there's no sense to it, Cougar.' D'Arcy urged the black on, and as weary as the horse was. It responded to the best of its ability. McGee had chosen a good animal when he had purchased this one from . . .

McGee — and that reminded D'Arcy of the promise he had made to Dallas. He had promised to finally tell Cougar about Reineke and Carlina. The murder. D'Arcy glanced at the big man across his shoulder and cursed silently. It was the last thing in the world he wanted to do, but he had promised Dallas. He had given his word to a dying man. Looking at Cougar now, D'Arcy wasn't even sure that the big scout could make it the short distance to the post. D'Arcy willed himself to break off that line of thinking and rode grimly on, concentrating only on guiding the faltering black horse toward the distant lights and muted music marking Fort Apache.

By the time D'Arcy could see the front gates distinctly, the music was ringing out clearly across the desert, and the black horse had foundered. It had given its best. The sentry atop the palisade watched the incoming riders cautiously and called out a challenge, lowering his rifle to the ready.

'Halt. Name and rank!' he boomed as he raised his Springfield rifle to his shoulder.

'Calvin D'Arcy. Here to see General Crook,' D'Arcy responded to the man whose face was lost in the shadow cast by the bill of his cap.

'That name don't mean a thing to me,' the sentry called back.

'I don't give a damn! Let us in.'

'No one passes after dark,' the sentry replied solidly.

'This is imperative, man!'

'That may be so, but I don't know you and my orders are that no one passes this gate after dark.'

'Open up, you fool!' Cougar bellowed hoarsely.

'I don't think so, I don't favor the stockade, friend,' the trooper answered stubbornly.

'I have a pass,' Cougar lied. 'Signed by General Plunkett.'

'I'd have to see it,' the soldier said dubiously.

'Then, damn you, come and see it!'

Cougar half-fell from the heaving horse's back and staggered to the judas gate. He could feel his wounded leg buckle with each step. D'Arcy sat the dying horse, watching.

Cougar withdrew the only piece of paper he had on him from his pocket — the German letter — and waited impatiently, leaning heavily against the unbarked logs of the stockade. From across the yard the band struck up a new tune. The sentry, or another, opened the small window in the gate and stared at Cougar for a long time.

'All right, if you got a pass, hand it over.' He thrust his hand out of the window and waited.

'My orders are to hand it over to no one. You can look at it — that's all you need to do,' Cougar said, holding the paper up. The guard squinted at it and growled.

'I can't read that in this light!'

'Then open the gate, damn you!'

Slowly the wheels in the trooper's mind turned over. The big man looked near to death, not much of a threat to anyone. The man on the black horse was staying well back. If that really was a pass from General Plunkett, the guard knew he would be in trouble for *not* letting them pass through.

'All right,' he finally decided, and the narrow judas gate opened ever so slightly. 'Now let me — '

But as soon as a hand appeared, Cougar grabbed it, his wild strength coming alive. Kicking at the gate, he managed to bring his other fist up and over, slamming it into the face of the soldier, whose warning cry was broken off in his throat by the force of the blow.

Cougar shouldered the gate open, stepping over the fallen trooper, drew his Colt and staggered forward. Stumbling toward the bar that secured the main gate he slid it free and swung the gate open, waving D'Arcy forward. From the parapet a warning shot rang out, splintering the log near Cougar's head. A voice cried out a warning from the near watchtower. Soldiers burst from the barracks and the door to the assembly hall was flung open. Officers from within rushed at the sound of the alert. Calvin D'Arcy rode toward them on the staggering black horse, waving his hat in the air and yelling.

And Solon Reineke shot him from his horse's back.

Reineke stood on the plankwalk in front of the assembly hall, smoking pistol in his hand, Field Marshal Von

Etzinger beside him. The Prussian whispered a frantic question and Reineke hissed back an answer.

'What in bloody hell is going on?' It was General Crook himself who yelled the question. He stood in his dress uniform, saber in his hand, glaring out at the disturbance in the night. A guard from the parapet shouted back an answer.

'Intruders, sir! It looks like they killed Corporal Dodd.'

Crook looked to D'Arcy lying sprawled dead on the ground and then to Reineke. 'Secure the gate!' he commanded his troopers. Officers and the few women from the ball crowded the plankwalk now in general confusion. The blaring band had fallen to instant silence. The trooper on the parapet called down a warning.

'Be careful, sir! There were two of them.'

And Carroll Cougar came limping toward them, stumbling out of the darkness into the lantern light from within. Crook, seeing the pistol in Cougar's hand, called out, 'Shoot him down!' as Ellen White screamed and screamed.

6

Ellen's eyes were fixed on the fearsome, sunburned interloper as he approached the group standing in front of the hall, and despite his ragged appearance and the poor light, she knew him instantly.

'It's Cougar!' she shouted, grabbing General Crook's arm impetuously. 'For God's sake, it's Carroll Cougar and D'Arcy.'

'Hold your fire!' Crook yelled, countermanding himself, but before the words were out of his mouth, Solon Reineke, gambling desperately, had fired again. The shot was too hasty by far. The bullet whipped past Cougar, spinning off into the night as it missed its target.

They all heard Cougar shout something brokenly, but no one later could say what it was. Ellen was sure it was 'Carlina!' No matter — Solon Reineke never heard it, or if he did it was the last thing he ever heard on this earth, for if his shot had missed, Cougar's did not. The .44 slug from the big man's revolver ripped through Reineke's throat, spattering those around him with blood as he toppled backward, his eyes wide and unbelieving, to die on the plank-walk. Another woman screamed. Rebecca Pointer fainted.

With all eyes on Reineke now, no one saw the Prussian unbutton the flap on his pistol holster and draw his Mauser.

No one, that is, but Cougar, who had been watching for just such a move. As the mustached Prussian field marshal drew his weapon, Cougar fired his Colt for the second time and the little popinjay took a heart shot. Von Etzinger stood, his gun dangling from his limp fingers, looking down in amazement at his previously impeccable uniform. Now blood spouted through it from a small, smoldering hole beneath his breast pocket. He lifted confused eyes to Cougar and then toppled forward, falling from the plankwalk head-first on to the hard-packed dirt of the parade ground.

Crook himself flinched and stepped back. Then he leveled a finger at Cougar and demanded, 'Just what in hell is this!'

Cougar did not answer the bearded general. He lifted an apologetic hand and fell over, crumpling against the earth with Ellen's scream still echoing in his ears as he tumbled down a long, long stone chimney in the desert to lie among the bones of the dead mountain sheep.

When Cougar again climbed up out of the terrifying chimney, he saw the pale, small hand of Ellen reaching toward him and she took his big, meaty hand in hers. He was afraid of falling into the chimney again, and he said, 'Don't let go.'

'No,' she promised. 'I won't. Not ever.'

Smiling, trusting her word, Cougar re-entered the cosmic darkness. When he again came to, the light was cutting, slanting through the sheer curtains on the window and Cougar winced. The brilliant glare was nearly painful after the long darkness he had suffered through.

Ellen had promised, and she was there, holding his hand. Cougar squinted up at her sitting there calmly, her jaw-line and cheekbones beautifully formed, her eyes closed, long lashes sheltering them. As if she could feel him looking at her, those eyes blinked open and her head turned toward him.

'How long was I gone?' he asked her in a raspy voice.

'Two days.'

'Two!' He tried to sit up in bed and failed. 'I've got to report to General Crook.'

'D'Arcy already has,' Ellen said, pushing him back gently.

'D'Arcy? How?'

'He was wounded, but not badly. You were in much worse shape than he was. He talked to Crook and gave him the letter from the President. Since then,

Crook has sent out forces against the Apaches, but found them dispersed again for the most part. The Prussians abandoned their materiel and fled to Mexico. It's over, Cougar. All you have to do is rest.'

'I missed it all,' he said ruefully. 'Reineke, though? He is dead?'

'He is.'

'Then . . .' Then nothing, he could rest now. That was done. He had Ellen, and the demon had been exorcised. Sleep, he did then, deeply. When he awoke next he was ravenously hungry and Ellen allowed him a little broth and some bread although he complained vehemently that he needed meat.

'There's time enough for that,' she said. 'Just now your body probably wouldn't accept it. By the way,' she said, 'D'Arcy has been anxious to see you.'

'Any time.'

'Now?' Ellen asked. 'He's outside, waiting.'

'Now's fine,' Cougar said, placing his

empty bowl on the table beside the bed. 'You could fill that again for me, if there's more.'

She smiled and promised, 'I will.' Then Ellen went out, and after a minute, Calvin D'Arcy appeared in the sunshine-bright oblong of the open doorway. Or was this D'Arcy? He wore his arm in a sling. His cheeks were sunken, his face very pale. He entered the room, closing the door behind him. D'Arcy's steps were uncertain as he crossed to Cougar's bed. He looked ten years older.

'Hello, Cougar,' D'Arcy said, drawing up a chair. He took his hat off and sat beside the bed. 'Are you hurtin' much?'

'Not too bad now. How about you, Calvin?'

'Mostly I'm stiff,' D'Arcy replied. Then he was silent for a long, long time, looking out the window. There was something on his mind obviously, but what?

'Are you going to tell me, Calvin?'

Cougar asked and D'Arcy seemed to nearly leap from his seat at the question.

'Tell you what?' D'Arcy said evasively.

'Whatever it is that you're trying to keep from me,' Cougar said with a smile. 'I've known you a long time, Calvin.'

'Yeah, you have,' D'Arcy answered. Again, however, he held his silence for a time. Finally, returning his eyes to Cougar's battered face, he took a long, deep breath and spoke. 'I promised McGee, you see, before he died. Otherwise I wouldn't have . . .'

'Promised Dallas what?' Cougar said impatiently. 'Damnit, Calvin, no guessing games, please. My head isn't up to them yet.'

'All right. It's just that it's hard to get started. I promised to finally tell you about Reineke and how Carlina died.'

'What do you mean? You're not going to try telling me that Solon didn't do it!'

D'Arcy lifted a hand. 'Of course he did, Carroll. He killed her — I saw it . . . only it was in self-defense.'

'It was *what*? Are you crazy, D'Arcy? What are you talking about?'

'Just what I said. Solon Reineke shot Carlina in self-defense. Do you remember hearing two shots that evening?' Cougar nodded. His eyes were intent now, half-closed as he recalled that night. 'Yes, two shots,' D'Arcy continued. 'And the first one was Carlina's.'

'You're not making any sense. This is all crazy,' Cougar objected. 'You say that Reineke shot Carlina but only because she had fired a gun at him?'

'That's right,' D'Arcy said without expression. His eyes didn't waver.

'That's insane,' Cougar growled. 'Why would she shoot him, D'Arcy? Why?'

'That's the hard part about telling you, Cougar,' D'Arcy sighed. He rose to walk to the window. Turning his back to Cougar he looked out across the long, clean desert, and Cougar could see the rigidity in his friend's back.

'Tell me, D'Arcy.' Whatever it was, he had to know, needed now to know.

'She shot because she was in my bed with me, damn you, Cougar!' D'Arcy shouted, and he spun toward Cougar, his eyes wild with mingled emotions, fear among them. 'Because you were out hunting and she came to my bed and crawled in.'

'I don't believe it.' Cougar's mouth was dry. His heart was thudding heavily. He kept his eyes fixed on D'Arcy, his killing eyes.

'Believe it, dammit! She was in bed with me and Reineke found us. Carlina was afraid he would tell you and so she grabbed my Colt and fired wildly. She missed and Reineke drew and fired back at the muzzle flash, not even knowing who had shot at him or why. The bullet killed her.'

'If that's so, why did Reineke take off, then?' Cougar asked weakly. He found himself believing D'Arcy, not wanting to believe him.

'Why?' D'Arcy broke into wild laughter. 'What would you have done to him if you had caught him on that night, the way you were? Came back and found her shed of her petticoats and Reineke with a fired pistol. He took off because he was scared to death of Carroll Cougar. The same reason I'm taking off. I've got a horse saddled outside. I'm leaving right now. You won't be out of bed for two or three more days. That'll give me time to get my start.'

'You recruited me and got me to come tracking all this way . . . knowing that Solon Reineke never did it?' Cougar asked in disbelief. 'Knowing that I was trying to kill a man out of vengeance when he never did the killing on purpose?'

'That's right,' D'Arcy said clearly.

'Why! Why, Calvin? Tell me!'

'For my country, Cougar. I knew mentioning Solon Reineke was one sure way to bring you tracking, and we needed you. I might be a bastard,

Cougar — but I do love my country and I had to balance that against using you. You know which was more important.' D'Arcy turned toward the door, hat still in his hands. He stopped and turned as he put it on. His hand was on the doorknob when he said, 'Carlina was no good, Cougar. No good at all.'

Then D'Arcy was gone. He heard Calvin say something to Ellen, heard her answer, and then the front door was drawn to. Cougar remained lying in stunned disbelief, his hands clenched, staring at the blank ceiling over his bed. He didn't even hear Ellen when she entered.

Twice she had to say, 'Here's more of that barley broth, Carroll.'

'Just put it down, will you, Ellen?'

Frowning, she did as he asked, wiping her hands on her apron. She asked, 'Is something wrong, Carroll?'

'Nothing much. It's just that D'Arcy brought a few ghosts by.'

'He's riding out; did he tell you?'

Ellen asked, sitting in the bedside chair.

'He told me.'

'He wouldn't say where he was going.'

'No. It doesn't matter. Wherever he's going, I won't be seeing him again.' Then he reached out and took Ellen's hand. He was going to sleep again for just a little while, and then he would need her hand to shoo away the ghosts if they came back haunting.

By the time he was able to sit up at the table and eat meat, the ghosts had mostly gone. He had come to grips with it — he had made a mistake, that was all. And he wasn't the first man to make that particular one. He had believed Carlina Polk to be as virtuous as she was beautiful. Perhaps that had come from not knowing too many good women in his time. Unfortunately he had let thoughts of her linger, let his sorrow and need for revenge cloud his life. Now, pottering around the kitchen as he ate, humming softly, was the woman who had brought the sunlight to break through those dark clouds of anger.

He had no hatred left to expend. Reineke had gotten what he deserved after all, even if Cougar's motive had been the wrong one. Neither could he work up any anger against D'Arcy. He certainly wasn't going to go tracking the man. He had better places to go, much better, and he wasn't going to risk his chance of getting there.

The lady had said yes.

★ ★ ★

Under a desert sky where stars by the thousands had been poured out, they had gone walking, his mouth trying to form the right words until finally he just stopped, took both of her hands and blurted it out.

'I've still got my ranch on Twin Creek, you know?'

'I know you do,' she said, looking down.

'It's not much to look at.'

'It doesn't have to be.' She lifted her eyes now and met his gaze as her hands squeezed his tightly. He could feel that she was trembling although the night was warm. Or was that him who was shaking?

'I was going to add another room on,' he said, continuing in a rush. I haven't got around to it yet.'

'You will. In time.'

'And I was going to dig a well, too.'

'That'll be fine when you do.'

'The town's not that far away.'

'That's good.'

'It's not much of a town.'

'It doesn't need to be.'

'Maybe we should find the chaplain,' he said, looking back toward the post.

'I guess maybe we should, Carroll Cougar,' had been her answer.

And together they had walked back. Twenty paces along Cougar stopped again, murmured, 'I do love you, Ellen,' and kissed her before they walked on.

* * *

Now Ellen turned from the stove in the Pointers' quarters. 'That's all the cleaning I'm going to do,' she said, untying her apron. 'If we mean to hit the trail before it gets too hot.'

Cougar rose heavily from the table and walked to Ellen, putting his hands briefly on her shoulders. 'How did you know you wanted me, Ellen?' he asked. 'Right off, I mean?'

Ellen laughed. 'A woman doesn't know why, always, Carroll. She just knows. I knew and that's all there was to it.'

In half an hour Cougar had the horses saddled, the pack animal ready to travel with their few belongings tied down. Holding the reins, he called toward the open doorway, 'It's time to go, Mrs. Cougar.'

Ellen looked around the Pointer place once more, seeing to it that they'd left nothing behind, and then after a quick stop to say goodbye to Mrs. Pointer and to thank the lieutenant for taking them in, they rode out through the main gate on to the broad morning desert.

General Crook had ridden out himself earlier in the day with a company of men hunting for any remnants of Fox Ring's band, but none of that meant anything to Cougar anymore. In time the Apaches would be subdued. In time the dreams of Quiet Star and her husband would vanish like smoke. It was inevitable. Yet Cougar would not be here to witness it. It would be something he would read in a newspaper years from now, something far away, an old memory nearly lost in the mists of time.

They rode long that day, but frequently they stopped, once beside a narrow waterfall and once in a grove of cottonwoods where cicadas sang in the warmth of the day. At sundown Cougar found a place to camp and while he saw to the care of the horses and started a small fire, Ellen stood on the ridge, watching color flood the valley.

Cougar slipped up beside her, and

for a while he just watched her standing there, transfixed, the light of sundown playing on her beautiful face.

'Will you miss this country, Ellen?' he asked, putting his arm around her waist.

'I don't know.' She smiled up at him and rested her head against his shoulder. 'That's strange, isn't it? This desert has treated us so horribly, but there is a beautiful aspect to it, a wild loneliness like no other place I have ever seen. The strange, volcanic calderas, the long white playas, the jutting red mesas.'

'You are right. It is a strange and lovely place,' Cougar agreed. 'There are no sunsets like desert sunsets, no place where the stars are so thick and close they seem like a silver carpet.'

'And there is yet snow on the high peaks above the terrible emptiness of the desert floor with its sidewinders and gila monsters. I think that, yes, in a way I shall miss it. Will you, Carroll?'

'In the way you mean, yes. I will miss it, but not deeply and not for a time. One day, perhaps, when it has become a more hospitable place, we will come back.'

'And we will bring the children to see it,' she said definitely, turning to face him, her arms circling his waist as she looked up into his rugged, loving face.

'Yes,' Cougar agreed, 'we will bring the children.'

7

At night they slept in lean-tos when it was time to make camp, or if there were no handy trees, in the open air beneath the many-colored stars and waning golden moon. Cougar would often stay awake much longer than Ellen, listening to the far-off howl of the coyotes, the hooting of a near owl, staring at the glimmering sky.

Most frequently he would lie propped up on one elbow, just looking down at the beautiful face of the woman he loved. How softly she breathed, how small and perfectly formed she was.

At last, it seemed, the cougar had been tamed. Not by force, but by sweetness and love. When he did awake, he would often find her up before him, boiling coffee, watching the curling flames as she fed small twigs into the fire. She would be humming then, or singing softly, and he ached with love. How he wanted to be home again with her, to build for her a finer house, to one day hear her humming in the morning to the baby in her arms.

'There are no Apaches in this country?' Ellen asked one morning as they rode through a wide valley where the grass was long and green and the wildflowers still bloomed, where scattered pine and cedars encircled the meadows.

'No. Not here. We've left their territory far behind.'

Only once, two days earlier, had Cougar seen any Apaches, and he had not told her then for fear of worrying her. It was a small band, moving southward toward Mexico.

He did not know if it was his imagination that caused him to think that he saw a single woman among that band turn her horse and ride to higher ground to watch as Cougar and Ellen drifted eastward. He did not know if that had been Quiet Star watching them go, but he liked to believe that it had been.

'I asked only because I was still a little afraid,' Ellen said.

'I know. There's nothing to fear now.'

'I was only a little afraid,' she repeated. 'So long as I have you, Carroll Cougar, what could truly frighten me?'

'Have I never frightened you, Ellen?' Cougar asked.

'No, not ever,' she replied. 'Only when I thought you were lost to me.'

They rode on, talking low lovers' talk, of what they would do at the ranch, of how Cougar should show his new wife off to his neighbors, of how many children they would have, what their names would be, if the boy should have a pup.

Tree squirrels scrambling from branch to branch, chattered around them as they passed through a pine grove; deer bounded away or stood motionless, watching their slow passing. A black bear, seated like one of his circus cousins, simply continued to feast on its blackberries, accepting their presence. They too belonged to the land, did they not?

Theirs was no long ride, but a honeymoon among the natural, the beautiful.

'I'll be sorry to see this journey end,' Ellen said one night as they lay in their bed.

'Will you? I'd have thought you were plenty tired of riding.'

'Oh, that. Yes.' She waved a hand. 'But it seems we are only two drifting children needing nothing but ourselves for perfect happiness, wanting no company. I know it will end, that it must! But I shall be sorry when these days are ended.'

'Maybe we should ride back to the desert again,' Cougar teased. 'Start over.'

'No, no, no!' she said. 'I always speak too soon. I do want to be home, Cougar. To be home and be at peace. With you.'

Her eyes were dancing in the starlight. Serious and amused at once. A different sort of light, one from within, came into them and she drew Cougar down to kiss her.

It was not much further, three days' travel at the most, to home, and now the land around them was richer, greener. They found a small brook and bathed in it. Refreshed, cooled, they rode on. Crossing the meandering brook, they rode into timber again. They had dipped down into a hollow and up the other side through a cloud of yellow butterflies when the four men came out of the pine-tree forest to block their path.

'Hold up there!' one of them commanded, and he made his demand from behind the sights of a Winchester repeater. He was a big, burly, bearded man with missing front teeth. The men flanking him were dirty as well, neither young nor old, all heavily armed.

'Matthew!' Ellen gasped, and Cougar glanced at her in surprise.

'Glad you still remember me, Miss White,' the man behind the Winchester said.

'Who are they, Ellen?' Cougar asked, his eyes combing them darkly.

'Look at their wrists,' she said, and he did so, seeing the bracelets they wore — the strange, braided bracelets of silver and gold wire.

'The Brotherhood,' Cougar said, understanding. Members of her father's failed church who rightly or wrongly believed that he had robbed them of their donated money.

'Yes,' the one called Matthew said. 'Unfortunately, all there are left of us after you killed one of our brothers and the Indians the others. But I don't hold that against you, big man. That was all Doctor White's fault. All we want is to get the gold back!'

'It's gone. Lost,' Ellen told him. 'Father — '

'Don't lie,' Matthew said savagely.

'My wife doesn't lie, and she isn't lying now,' Cougar told him and his voice was as hard and unpolished as raw steel.

'Your wife . . . ? I see — well, that

doesn't matter, either. If you don't have the gold with you, you must know where it is.'

'We don't have it with us, I promise you,' Cougar said as his horse shifted its feet slightly. 'The Apaches have it. If you want to trail after them to ask them about it, I can tell you where they've gone.'

'I believe we'll have to take a look in your pack,' Matthew said.

'If it'll satisfy you,' Cougar said through tight lips, 'but what I just told you is the truth.'

'Luke,' the leader of the Brotherhood said to one of his men, 'see if there's gold in that pack,' and a lean, long-nosed man nodded, kneeing his horse forward. As Cougar watched, Luke spilled their pack on to the ground, got down and toed through it, finding nothing.

'Not here, Matthew. Maybe they hid it somewhere.'

'We told you what happened to it!' Ellen exclaimed.

'Fine,' Matthew said, leaning forward across his horse's withers. 'Now I'm telling you this — that's our gold. Your father bilked us out of it for that crazy temple he was supposed to build. I don't know how he ever got us to believe in all of that stuff. He sure never brought my brother, Martin, back to life, as he said he could, did he?'

'Ellen had nothing to do with any of that,' Cougar said.

'She's his daughter, and she knows where he hid that gold.'

'How many times do we have to tell you?' Ellen wailed. 'The Indians have it! Father ran off with the wagon and they ambushed him. Just go home, Matthew; leave us alone, can't you?'

'Not after all we've been through, not after seeing more of our friends die over it, no. We'll have the truth about the gold. Where did you hide it? Truth!'

'It is the truth,' Cougar said with icy weariness. 'Spin those horses of yours around and get out of here.'

'I don't think so. You know where the

gold is, big man. *Sure* — you're her husband, right! You know. You go and get it, Mr. And we'll just keep Ellen here until you come back with it. Don't worry, we'll take good care of her.' His smile was wolfish enough to bring panic into Ellen's eyes, a small, choked cry to her lips.

'You'd best do what I asked, friend,' Carroll Cougar warned Matthew and the others solemnly.

'No, Mr. This is our game, understand!'

Matthew shifted his rifle slightly and Cougar drew and fired in one motion, his bullet plowing through Matthew's skull, ripping the top of his head off. Cougar spun, shooting down the man called Luke as he stood like a jackal over their small packet of belongings. As the man to Cougar's left drew his gun, Cougar kicked his horse forward, spoiling the Brotherhood man's aim. Cougar shot him square in the face.

The last one hesitated too long, deciding whether to throw up his hands and surrender or fight. By the time he went for his gun, Cougar's pistol had swung around toward him, and he shot the last of the Brotherhood in the heart twice, watching without remorse as the man toppled from his saddle and fell to the pine-needle-covered earth.

Then there was nothing but the rolling smoke, the faint echo of the gunfire from the far hills and Ellen's crying sounds. He backed his horse beside her and held her tightly as she sobbed.

'Can we go home now, Cougar?' she asked, lifting her tear-streaked face to him, and he kissed each eye lightly.

'Sure. Let me remake our pack and we'll be on our way.'

As they started on the birds had already begun to sing again as if they knew that life was meant for joyous things.

8

The homecoming was not as glorious as these things are always imagined beforehand. From the forested knoll overlooking the house and yard of the Twin Creek ranch, the glitter of the sunlit stream as it flowed through the oaks was beautiful. There was new grass on the low hills surrounding the house and a few flowers — blue gentians and black-eyed Susans — had begun to lift their faces toward the bright sun. Riding down into the little valley, Carroll Cougar could feel his heart swelling with pride of ownership, with relief at having gotten home once more, with pride in the young wife he had accompanying him.

When he had purchased the place, after his first tour of duty with Crook, it had been done only as a refuge, a place to hide away from the war, the world

— both of which he had had more than enough of. It had never been a home in the true sense.

Now it was his home, a place where he would happily work and live out his days with the help and comfort of Ellen. They emerged from the trees on to the flat land and Cougar immediately began to scowl. Nothing was as he remembered it.

A section of the horse corral was torn down, the posts lying on the ground to rot. Had he done that himself? He tried to remember. In his rush to leave the property to go after Solon Reineke and reach General Crook, he had hurriedly hied his spare horses from the enclosure and driven them to the small town nearby, which had no known name but most in the area called Badger Crossing. He and Calvin D'Arcy had driven the horses to sell to a man Cougar knew named Joe Compton.

Cougar knew he hadn't been thinking too clearly just then; his rage had not permitted logical thought.

He might well have simply torn down a section of the corral. He cared nothing for his own property at that moment. There was a brief, mad thought of burning his own house, he recalled, figuring that he would never return to it — or be able to.

He was grateful now that he hadn't given in to that wild impulse, yet he continued to wear a frown. The house, so solid and appealing in memory, now appeared forlorn and crumbling. The front porch sagged like a sway-back mule; one of the uprights could be seen to be splintered. There were shingles loose on the roof. Never having been painted, the walls were weathered and gray.

Cougar halted his horse and sat silently, studying the house.

'What is it, Carroll?' Ellen asked. 'What's wrong?'

'The place. The place is all wrong, Ellen. It looks like some empty, abandoned shack.'

'Well, that's what it was, Carroll. It

has been empty since you abandoned it. Now you're back and I'm with you. It won't ever be empty again, because we will fill it up with our love, and it won't be abandoned again, will it?'

She smiled, touching his forearm. 'I didn't expect it to be perfect, but everything can be fixed again — unless you've forgotten how to drive a nail and I no longer know how to sweep and use a paintbrush.'

'There's liable to be a mess inside as well,' Cougar told her. 'When I left I was a little out of control. A few things were thrown.'

'We'll pick them up again,' Ellen said softly. 'Maybe for now we ought to swing down and go in and see where we plan to start. For myself, I've had enough of saddles.'

Cougar looked at his new wife, wondering at her thoughtful concern, her readiness to get to work to provide a home for them. She had courage as well, Cougar knew that. She had proven it along the trail. He could only nod; his emotions were nearly overflowing.

'You're right, of course. Let's get doing. Nothing's ever accomplished by wishing it done; there's no need to sit regretting something that you can fix just by moving, is there?'

'Tomorrow,' Ellen said before they swung down. 'Tomorrow is soon enough to start doing. Today, show me all around the place. We'll find something to make dinner of and go to bed early. How's that sound?'

'Blessed,' Carroll Cougar said.

Inside the house things were worse than he had imagined. A table and chair he had upset upon leaving still lay where they had fallen. He picked them up and repositioned them. The dust on the plank floor was heavy and thick. There must have been a windstorm at some time, and Cougar had negligently left two windows open in the back of the house — closing his windows was the last thing he would have been thinking about at the time.

The chimney would likely have been

taken over by owls or raccoons or other small pests. It would have to be cleaned. Was there anything at all in the larder to make a meal of? Anything that had not gone bad? He had no idea. Walking to the kitchen, leaving boot prints in the dust, he startled a rat scurrying across the floor.

'Filthy things,' Cougar said. 'I hate them.'

'It probably wasn't too happy to see you,' Ellen said, maintaining her sense of humor in the face of what Cougar saw as ruination. Carroll Cougar paused. He turned toward Ellen, taking her shoulders in his large, callused hands.

'Thank you, Ellen.'

'For what?' she asked, smiling as she cocked her head to look up at his face.

'For not being too disappointed, for being willing to work with me to repair things, for making my mood just a little easier.'

'Cougar,' she said, 'I'm your wife — those are things I'm supposed to do.'

'Not all women would . . .'

'No, I suppose not all women would — and it's to their own misfortune. Look, Carroll, the way I look at it is I have a house, a husband who loves me. Why would I not want to please the man and work to make my home better?'

Cougar wagged his head heavily. 'Ellen, for the sake of other men I hope that you are not the last of your kind.'

Ellen rose to her toes and kissed Cougar's forehead. 'For the sake of other women, Carroll Cougar, I hope that you are not the last of *your* kind. Now, let's keep looking around; what else needs to be done?'

Cougar opened the back door off the kitchen and promised to put up a clothes line in the yard. Ellen was already planning a vegetable garden and a small flower plot. Cougar left the back door open for fresh air. He wasn't worried about small critters coming in; it seemed they were already there.

The bedroom was a bachelor's. Raw, clothes strewn across the floor, two rough blankets tossed on the unmade bed, which had no linen. He had never purchased such things in his life. There was little use for sheets on the long trail. Seeing it through Ellen's eyes, Cougar was for the first time ashamed of the way he had been living. She crossed to the window and seemed to be visually measuring it for curtains — after the room was swept and painted.

'There's a lot of work to be done, isn't there?' Cougar asked.

'It doesn't have to all be done today, in a week, a month. I'm planning on us being here for a long, long time — unless you get the urge to go tracking again.'

'No, that day will never come, Ellen. What do you want to do now?'

'You could show me around outside. I want to know the whole ranch.'

'It's hardly a ranch. I've got a nice little eighty-acre parcel. Since I never meant to raise stock, I figured that would do me.'

'I figure it will do me, too. Can we look around?'

The sun was still high and bright, the

skies clear. There was a cool breeze stirring the upper reaches of the oaks and swaying the willows along the creek. They walked that way. If Cougar could no longer feel much pride in his house, still he took pleasure in the natural setting of the place. The river flowed pleasantly past, silver-bright. A cluster of redwing blackbirds sang in the willows. A lone eagle soared on the air currents high above; the foothills, green with new grass, crowded the north side of the valley. Ellen grabbed Cougar's arm to halt him and she pointed toward the riverbank where a doe and her two spotted fawns drank.

'That makes me think about the supper we haven't got,' Cougar said.

'Oh, Cougar, you wouldn't shoot her, would you?' Ellen asked with genuine concern.

'I was just teasing you,' Carroll Cougar answered. 'Besides, I haven't got my rifle with me.'

He indicated the flatter land to the east and explained that was where his horses had been allowed to roam when they were not penned. 'There's no place they can really wander there, not with the hills rising. Besides, they never were of a mind to. They had everything they could want right here.'

Ellen leaned against his shoulder and smiled up. She said nothing aloud, but her look seemed to say that she had all she could need right here as well.

Back at the house Ellen tied a scarf over her head and pulled out the old broom she found in the utility closet. 'I'll feel better if I at least start somewhere,' she told Cougar.

'That's what I should be doing as well,' Cougar agreed. 'Just start, then something will be accomplished on this day.'

'Any idea where you'll begin?' Ellen asked.

'It's probably not the most necessary, having only the two horses, but I think I'll raise the corral again. It's been on my mind to do so; it will make the whole yard look better. Maybe I'll whitewash it tomorrow. There should still be a batch of that in the shed.'

'That would be prettifying,' Ellen said. 'And Cougar, don't worry about starving to death. I found a sack of dried beans the critters hadn't gotten to and some tinned condensed milk, and some cornmeal. If you'll bring in some kindling wood sometime today I can fix us a mess of cornbread and beans to eat.' Apologetically, Ellen said, 'I know it's not much to offer . . . '

'Anything is a lot to offer a man when he's hungry. Besides,' he smiled, 'it's about all we have until I can get into Badger Crossing, which I intend to do tomorrow. You'll have to come along and help me with the shopping.'

'Can we afford it?' Ellen asked with some concern.

'Ellen, believe it or not the army actually does pay its men. I've enough, and it's either we spend it on food or put you on a diet of venison.'

Again Ellen was not sure if Cougar was kidding or not. The man would take some getting used to. Well, wasn't that what honeymoons were about? And as strange as it had been, this was their honeymoon. Cougar said, 'I'd better bring the wood in first, then you can let those beans boil while we work.'

'That's what I was thinking,' Ellen agreed. 'I'll always be around to stir them while I'm sweeping.'

'Ellen,' Cougar said, holding his wife. 'Just don't get yourself overtired trying to do everything at once.' There was a teasing glint in his eyes.

'I won't get myself that tired,' she promised. Then she kissed him once and got to work. She was putting a big black iron pot on the stove when Cougar stepped outside to see what kindling he could gather from beneath the oaks. He made it about four strides from the house before a hidden rifle cracked and a bullet whipped past Cougar's head, near enough to hear.

Cougar sprinted for the shelter of the oak trees. He rolled to the ground beside a big old specimen and drew his

Colt. He still had not been carrying his Spencer rifle — an old habit he had shrugged off as if there could be no troubles in his new life. He had forgotten temporarily that there was a reason he carried his rifle, had it near him at all times.

The concealed rifleman fired again, a Winchester or a Henry he was using, Cougar could tell from the sharp crack of the weapon. The second bullet slammed into an oak tree, spraying Cougar with bark, making a groove across the white meat of the tree. But it was not the tree that Cougar had sheltered behind. The ambusher had lost his quarry in the tangled shadows of the oak grove.

Cougar tried not to move, not to give the sniper a better target, but he had seen Ellen appear on the front porch of the house, looking in all directions. Even at that distance Cougar could see how agitated she was. He waved her frantically back into the house, fearing that the movement would bring another, nearer shot, but none came. Perhaps that was because the would-be assassin now recognized that there was another person in the house, and if Cougar was not carrying his .56 Spencer, the other person had it to hand.

For whatever reason the attacker had withdrawn, or so Cougar believed. He was in no hurry to test his theory. For another long hour he lay on his belly in the oak grove, watching and listening. Then he rose, brushed the leaf litter from his buckskin shirt and blue jeans. He planted his old cavalry hat and since he was already among the trees, gathered what dry wood he could find to start Ellen's stove burning. He circled the house, using the back door of the kitchen to enter. He whistled soundlessly as was his habit of many years and stacked the wood. Ellen had rushed to the kitchen to watch him. She said nothing, but her terror was obvious in her expression.

Cougar put on his best smile, rose and went to her, holding his new bride in his arms, feeling her trembling.

'Oh, Cougar,' she muttered into his chest, 'is it all going to start again?'

'No, it's not. That was probably nothing — a hunter with a bad shooting eye.'

Ellen did not believe that, nor did Cougar. One bullet could be a randomly discharged careless shot, but not two. 'We'd better get to work, Ellen, or we won't get anything done today.'

'Surely you're not going back out there!' she protested.

'Surely I am. I can't accomplish much in here.' He added to the frightened woman, 'Besides, no man is going to drive me from my own property. That's been tried.'

It had been. A man named Trace Fenner had sold Cougar the Twin Creek property in a moment of financial distress, but always believed somehow that he still held moral title. He and his sons had come looking for Cougar to reclaim the property, a decision which had not ended well for the three of them.

'Where'd you put my rifle, Ellen?'

'It's on the bed — put it there while I was cleaning under it.' Cleaning *under* a bed? The ways of women were mysterious and marvelous. 'There's another one hanging right over the fireplace,' she pointed out.

Yes, his Winchester still hung on its stag-horn brackets, but it had not been cleaned and oiled since Cougar had gone looking for General Crook. One more task he had to add to his mental list — which had gotten quite long since returning. Besides, he favored his old Spencer. They had traveled many miles together, entered many battles. Its satisfying, deep-throated report had been enough to cow some other would-be gunmen. He would use the old Spencer until ammunition for it could not be found — which day was probably coming soon — the reason he had purchased the new Winchester repeater in the first place.

Over dinner, which was a satisfying

meal of beans with bacon from Cougar's traveling stores and golden cornbread, they discussed the day's small accomplishments. The corral had been erected once again and the house, or at least half of it, was dusted and swept. Ellen was still worried; it showed in her eyes. Finally she could stand it no longer. Pushing her plate aside she folded her hands together and asked Cougar: 'All right, Carroll, who was it? Who was trying to kill you?'

'I told you — '

'Yes, a blind hunter. This is not the time for false reassurances, Cougar. I need to know.' Her eyes were intent, her manner solemn. No, she would not be put off with an invented lie. Ellen suggested, 'Could it have been Fox Ring, Carroll? I don't think the Apache leader would ever give up.'

'Not on the battlefield,' Cougar agreed. 'But he wouldn't let a personal grudge drive him this far from his people. If you'll remember, we saw Fox Ring riding toward Mexico. He had

Quiet Star with him, They were looking for a place to start a new life, too.'

Cougar went on, 'Besides, I don't think Fox Ring would kill me from hiding. He would want to do it face to face. Any other way he would see as cowardly. No,' Cougar said, shaking his shaggy head. 'I can't believe it could have been Fox Ring.'

'Well, the Prussians, then. You ruined their plan and killed Field Marshal Von Etzinger as well.'

'No,' Cougar answered. 'For a different reason. They are soldiers trained to fight in a different way. Ten or twelve of them might have marched up to the house and assaulted it, but I don't think they would send a single soldier to do the work — not if they wanted to be sure that it was done.'

'So you assume it was not the Prussians, but you don't know it.'

'I just go by their past behavior as I do with Fox Ring,' Cougar said. 'Though I admit that anything is possible.'

'All right,' Ellen said with a sigh. Her

eyes were bright in the lantern light by which they had eaten their poor meal. 'Who else could you suggest? Who wants you dead that badly?'

'You're not forgetting the Brotherhood, are you? They still believe that you and your father stole the collection meant to establish a temple, and that we must know where the gold is.'

Ellen was briefly meditative before she answered, 'I think that Matthew and his friends we encountered along the trail were the last of them — the last who would trek so far to try to find the mythical money.'

'But we can't know that either, Ellen.'

'No.' She sighed again and reached across the table to touch Cougar's big hand. 'We can't be sure of that either. Are there any more possibilities? I never realized how many enemies we have made.'

'I wonder who took over the Fenner ranch,' Cougar said, musing. 'Trace Fenner still imagined he held a claim to my property. Maybe whoever took over the ranch believes that too — especially if they're family of his.'

'Whoever that is would think that you'd not only taken over the family's land but killed three of their clan.'

'Yes. Or if the deed was never registered, someone new might have purchased it and believed that the property included my ranch. They would see me as an interloper, a squatter, since they would know nothing of me or of my dealings with Fenner.'

'There's that to consider,' Ellen said thoughtfully. Her expression altered slightly. 'I have another possibility to suggest,' she said tentatively.

'Yes?' he encouraged.

'Carroll, have you considered another man who has reason to fear you enough to want you dead? Have you forgotten about Calvin D'Arcy?'

9

Cougar was taken aback at Ellen's suggestion. Of course he remembered Calvin D'Arcy. They had been through many battles together as army scouts for General Crook. They had been the best of trail-friends for a long, long time. Until . . .

Ellen said, 'He promised Dallas McGee as McGee lay dying that he would tell you the truth about Carlina, and he did. D'Arcy admitted that he had been sleeping with your woman.' Cougar only nodded; he did not want to revisit that painful part of his life ever again. Ellen was not through yet.

'Yet D'Arcy let you believe that Solon Reineke had murdered Carlina. When he finally did confess to you in your sickbed he left the fort, frightened out of his wits. He was sure that you would pursue him as you had Reineke. I saw him that day, Carroll, remember? He was trembling, eager only to run before you could track him down as well.'

'That's all done with now,' Cougar said, touching the back of Ellen's hand.

'Maybe it isn't over for Calvin D'Arcy, Cougar. Maybe fear of you has taken over his life so that he can think of nothing more than eliminating you from it.'

'You don't know D'Arcy like I do,' Cougar said, rejecting the possibility.

'As well as you once thought you knew him, you mean,' Ellen countered. 'Carroll, that man was panicked — I saw him as he left Fort Apache. He rode as if there was a devil on his heels and the devil was named Carroll Cougar.'

Cougar rose, pushing his heavy chair back away from the table. It was all too much to be considered on this night. He did not wish to consider anything but Ellen. The glint, Ellen saw, was back in his eyes. She rose, took his hand and followed him to the bedroom to enter the peace of a long, loving night.

Carroll Cougar was up early in the morning, leaving Ellen to linger in peaceful sleep for a while longer. The woman had been through a lot. He took down the Winchester rifle and partially disassembled it, cleaning and oiling the weapon. He did not intend to use it that day, but leaving it neglected seemed nearly sinful. Besides, there might come a day when he did need it — and that not far away.

The work eased Cougar's concern and seemed to help him focus his thoughts. He had to come up with a new plan. The work around the ranch would have to be held in abeyance. If he could not guarantee his own safety or Ellen's there, nothing could be accomplished.

It was as he placed the Winchester aside and begun cleaning his Spencer that he became certain of what he must do. He could not sit idly by while an unnamed enemy waited to kill him. Their shopping trip planned for that morning would have to wait. With a huge sigh, Cougar rose, glanced out the front window of his house and then toward the back room where Ellen slept.

He would have to earn his peace, it seemed, and the only way to do that was to find his would-be killer.

Ellen would not like it, and he could not blame her, but it was for her as well as himself that it must be done. He had to go out and find a man he did not know. Where he might be, Cougar did not know, but if he had to prowl the entire long country like a stalking big cat, then he would. It was time for the cougar to prowl.

Ellen emerged from the bedroom as Cougar was finishing reloading the Spencer .56. She wore a tender smile which became a yawn and then a frown.

'What are you doing, Carroll?'

'Just what it looks like, cleaning the rifles.'

'I guess what I meant is why are you

doing that?' she asked, sitting opposite him, sweeping her dressing gown between her knees and holding it there with both hands. Her look was genuinely inquisitive, but her eyes held a doubtful shadow.

Ellen's hair was loose in the morning. The sunlight through the east window cast her into splendid profile. Cougar could not lie to the woman, did not wish to. 'I won't be able to take you shopping today. There's something else I have to do.'

Ellen looked away, evading the truth. 'Well,' she answered, 'there's cornbread left from last night. I don't mind cornbread and coffee for breakfast. And if it comes to dinner, that pot of beans is still half full, so I'll be all right for today.' When she could dodge the question no longer, she asked with deep concern in her eyes, 'Where are you going, Carroll? What is it you mean to do?'

He fiddled with the box of cartridges on the table, putting the extra unneeded bullets back. He knew that he could not evade the point any longer. 'I'm going out to look for peace, Ellen.'

'What does that mean? Wait!' she said, holding up one hand. 'I think I know — you are taking to the trail again, tracking.'

'Not tracking. I told you there is no more of that for me. I just mean to have a look around.'

'Just sort-of go skulking?' Ellen said with a short laugh. She was still looking away from Cougar.

'More like prowling,' he said.

'I want to go along.'

'No, I don't want you to, Ellen.'

'So, that's that, then. Oh, well, I guess I'd better get used to being left alone, hadn't I?'

'It's not like that, Ellen,' Cougar said, rising to stand beside her. 'Not like the old days. My long travelling days are over. I promised you that. It's just that this is something I must do for the both of us. We are not safe on this place right now, and if we're not safe here at home, there's no place on earth we will ever be safe. You can avoid a rattlesnake for so long, but you know it's always there, somewhere in the long grass, or under the house. It has to be killed.'

'And who are you going to kill, Carroll?' Ellen asked, snuffling just a little as she looked up at him with moist eyes.

'I don't know,' he answered heavily. 'I don't know if it's one of the Fenners, the Prussians, the Brotherhood, Fox Ring or even Calvin D'Arcy. Maybe it's none of them; I don't know. But I have to find out because I mean for this house, this valley, to be our safe haven.'

'All right,' Ellen said, not without emotion, but with resignation. 'I suppose I understand, although I don't like it.'

'I don't like it much myself, but it's the only way, Ellen. It has to be done. We can't just wait for him to come again — whoever it is — and kill one of us from ambush.'

She nodded her head, unhappiness bowing her shoulders. The rat, or another just like it, scuttled across the floor, but Cougar paid no attention to it. He had other concerns.

'Where are you going to start?' Ellen asked.

'I'm going over to the Fenner house. I've never been there, not even when Trace Fenner and I were doing business together. We didn't exactly have a companionable relationship.'

'The man who sold you this property and then tried to take it back by force? Yes, I remember you telling me about it.'

'I think it's the place to start, for reasons we discussed last night. I'll look the place over, watching for tracks between our ranches on my way. Maybe I'll try to talk to someone over there — I don't know who lives there now, but maybe I can get a feel for whoever it is, what they want . . . if anything.'

'All right,' Ellen said. She had now regained her composure. There was no point in arguing; Cougar would do what he felt he must do anyway. 'Would you mind if later on I rode over to

Badger Crossing myself to purchase a few things?'

Cougar reflected. 'I suppose that would be all right. But, Ellen, I wouldn't mind if you wanted to tote the Winchester along.'

'If it will make you feel better, I will,' she said, rising. 'Although I should be safe. Anyone who knows you would know that harming me could only make things much worse for them.'

Cougar's own reasoning was that Ellen would be as safe on the well-traveled road to Badger Crossing as she would be alone in the house with an unknown killer around. She would be safer than she would be riding with him.

Carroll Cougar knew that he had become a marked man again.

Cougar saddled the gray horse he had been riding since Fort Apache, thought things over and then saddled Ellen's red roan as well. She might not be ready to ride out this early in the day, but he now found himself hoping that she would leave the house soon. No matter, the roan could stand to wear its saddle for a while. When Cougar led the gray from the corral, the roan wanted to go along as well. The two horses had traveled together for many a day. Many a mile.

When Cougar did swing into leather he could see Ellen peeking out the front window, and his heart sank. He did not wish to ever leave her in a situation like this again — but then, that was the purpose of his prowling: to get rid of the rattlesnake before it could become a constant threat to them. Cougar rode slowly out of the yard and on to the grassy flats. A horse's imprints would not take well on that ground. He might have had better luck tracking along the creek in that sandy soil, but if the rider had come from the Fenner place, there was no reason for him to follow the creek when it could be reached by a straight run across the long meadow.

The flats looked too empty now, isolated. In earlier times, Cougar had let his small herd of horses out here to graze and to wander freely. Some of the animals would romp up to meet Cougar when they saw him arriving with a hay wagon or simply looking around, counting heads. Well, he would build his horse herd again. He needed a couple of brood mares and a healthy stallion. Both the roan and the gray horse were geldings. Cougar thought he could afford a few horses. He mentally totaled the money he had been paid by the army, how much he would have to deduct from that to repair the house and keep it stocked with needed supplies.

It could be done. Cougar realized abruptly that he even had money deposited in the Badger Crossing bank — which was really just a strongbox in Stinky Barret's saloon — that he had left there over two years ago for safe keeping. He was not so poor as he had imagined.

Reaching the pass leading through the rank of grassy hills, Cougar rode through it, only occasionally glancing above him toward the rough country where a sniper could be hidden. There was no way anyone could have been expecting him to ride this way on this morning, and it seemed unlikely that someone would have posted sentries — still, you never knew.

At least, he told himself, he was not pursuing a band of Apaches, but only a single disgruntled man. Or so he had convinced himself. He knew that Trace Fenner was dead — for he had killed and buried the man himself, but with him gone an entire clan of Fenners could have moved into the house, taking over the once-prosperous ranch. Cougar had never asked if Fenner had more family around. It had never seemed important.

As the trail crested out, Cougar could see the two-story Fenner house. It was gray with white trim, the porch and eaves dripping with gingerbread decorations. Farther ahead Cougar could see the small, dark forms of a cattle herd grazing. There were only a hundred or so of them, no inconsiderable number but far fewer than Fenner had run in earlier times when he decided that he needed back the extra range that he had sold to Cougar.

Cougar rode down a winding trail toward the valley, his eyes continuing to search the land. He saw no one. Not a horseman appeared anywhere, which was odd on a working cattle ranch, but Cougar accepted the situation gratefully. Groups of men, strangers especially, asked tougher questions of a lone rider. Cougar had no wish to become engaged in some trivial, unnecessary altercation.

Approaching the gray house he still saw no one. There was a small white pony at the side of it, grazing on a bed of flowers. The pony lifted its head and looked toward Cougar, a red tulip dangling from its mouth. There were small misdemeanors occurring at all times everywhere. The pony did not seem to feel guilty at having been caught among the flowers. It continued to munch on them.

Cougar rode to the front steps where a white iron hitch rail stood. He waited a minute to see if anyone would appear at the door, and when no one did, he swung down, leaving his long gun in its scabbard. Stepping up on to the porch he crossed to the door and rapped on it loudly enough for anyone inside to hear.

Cougar waited for someone to answer, the cool wind working across his body, lifting the fringes of his buckskin jacket. He had raised his knuckles to knock again when the door suddenly swung open. A blonde woman of about thirty years of age, wearing a blue gingham dress, stood there. She could not be called beautiful, but she was a striking woman with high cheekbones and flat planes to her face. Her hair was styled carefully. Her lips formed a small smile. It was her eyes that Cougar did not like. These were as flat as some long-time lawman's, untrusting, cold. They were dark gray, the color of slate and reflected as much emotion.

'Yes?' was all she said.

'My name is Carroll Cougar,' he said in a rehearsed speech. 'I'm your neighbor from over at Twin Creek. I've been away for a while and thought I'd ride by and introduce myself.'

'Mr. Normand is not here. I'm sorry.'

Not knowing who Mr. Normand was, Cougar didn't know what to say. 'This used to be the Fenner ranch,' was all he could come up with.

'It still is. My name is Gloria Fenner. Earl Normand is my uncle — my mother's brother. If it is ranch business you're here to discuss, this is not the time. Mr. Normand has ridden off to Badger Crossing to take care of a few matters.'

'I see,' Cougar said, belatedly removing his old cavalry hat. 'Well, then — another time.' He nodded and feeling that he had been dismissed, walked down the three porch steps. Feeling some vague sense of responsibility he told her, 'There's a horse in your tulips.'

'I'll see to it,' Gloria Fenner said.

Cougar mounted the gray horse and sat there for a minute. Now what? He could wait for Mr. Earl Normand's return, but there was really not any point in it. He had just had the idea that he should get the feel of the mood on the Fenner ranch, but if Normand was as unforthcoming as Gloria Fenner he would learn little.

Maybe he should ride toward Badger Crossing himself. He might meet Normand on the trail. Or, he might be able to catch up with him in town. Cougar himself had things to do there. He wanted to talk to Joe Compton, if he was still around, about buying some horses. He also wanted to talk to little Stinky Barret who owned the saloon there to see if he still had Cougar's money stashed in his strongbox — if Stinky was still around. Men came and went, appeared out of nowhere and then disappeared forever out in the wild country. Cougar could only hope that Stinky and his money had not vanished as well.

Starting slowly from the yard in a thoughtful mood, Cougar was startled by the roar of a big-bored weapon. He flinched and leaned low over the withers of his equally startled horse. The report was that of a shotgun, Carroll recognized. Reaching for his sidearm, he turned in the saddle to see Gloria Fenner, a smoking twelve-gauge scattergun in her hands, watching as the white pony that had been in her flower bed scampered away. There was the thinnest of smiles on her lips as she turned back toward the house, hoisting her skirts.

Cougar watched until the lady was back in the house and had fastened the door.

It was not Cougar, but the miscreant pony she had been trying to frighten away. She had proven one thing to Cougar, however: the lady did know how to use a gun and was not shy about doing so.

The trail to Badger Crossing was not long, but unfamiliar to Cougar from this end. He walked the gray steadily, his eyes watching for any approaching rider. He had decided that he needed to talk to Earl Normand, but was concerned that open country might not be the best place to do so, not knowing Normand or his intentions. Was the ranch boss alone? There was no way of knowing that either. He might have had three men, a dozen, riding with him for some reason. There had been no working men at all visible on the Fenner ranch.

There was one more thing that Cougar could not puzzle out at the moment. It was frustrating in a way. He was not some sort of detective, but a straight-line man who liked to understand the situation and go at it directly. The present situation seemed to avoid definition, leaving Cougar without a direct course of action. He only knew that some faceless man wanted him dead, wanted to harm Ellen, and he had to find the snake before he could succeed in doing so. It was much simpler to have the enemy pointed out and attacking him, no matter the odds.

Cougar dragged into the tumbledown town of Badger Crossing somewhere around noon on that day, with the sun high, the skies clear and the air cool around him. The place was still familiar, but the faces of the men he passed were all those of strangers as he made his way along the rutted street. The town had no reasonable expectation of survival, but here it still stood. Although the whole place seemed to be tilting just a little.

The reasonable place to begin was at Stinky's saloon where Cougar could ask about his money and seek out Earl Normand, who, if he had arrived in town, must surely have gravitated toward Stinky's. There was no other place in the tumbledown town for men to meet, no other to buy a glass of clouded, green beer or a throat-scalding shot of Stinky's homemade whisky. Stinky had once told Cougar that it took about three shots of his liquor before a man came to appreciate it. Cougar had always thought that it took about three shots before a man could put the stuff away without his stomach rebelling as it hit bottom. It took some getting used to, that much was for sure.

Stinky Barret's saloon was a low-ceilinged, dismal place. A weathered gray building no paintbrush had ever touched, with the exception of the whitewashed, nearly illegible sign someone had painted on a plank and nailed up, which read, 'Stinky's Place'.

Cougar tied up the gray at the hitch rail, briefly scanning the other mounts there. He saw no familiar horses, no familiar brands. He unsheathed his Spencer and took it into the saloon with him. He didn't want to leave its fate to chance.

The interior of Stinky's was dark and gloomy, reflecting its clientele. Stinky's was not some wide-open, boozy place with men laughing and shouting, glasses breaking, like you might run across in Wichita or Abilene when the trail herds were in. The men drinking here were gray and solemn, mentally counting their own meager pocket money or the days left in their lonely lives, calculating how much whisky it would take to make such matters negligible.

Crossing the swayed floor, Cougar looked around, seeing only two familiar faces. Another man, a complete stranger, called out, 'You won't need that buffalo gun in here, friend!' Cougar ignored him and walked on toward the long plank resting across four beer barrels, which had always served as Stinky's bar.

There was a narrow-faced, pale man with a tic behind the counter. 'Is Stinky still around?' Cougar asked.

'Where else would I be, Cougar?' Stinky himself asked from behind him.

Stinky Barret was a very small man, not much over or under five feet tall. He always wore a gold-colored vest under his coat and a short red tie. He had some hair, not much, and a sparkling pair of blue eyes. The way Stinky himself told it, he had been a gold-rush

158

adventurer in California, exhausting himself at that rough trade. One day, deciding that he had had enough and that he would die out there if he did not leave the work to younger, stronger men, Stinky had started for home in Louisiana, but he never made it. Exhausted from his labors, ready to fall off of his horse, Stinky decided to remain where he was — wherever that was — and use his remaining gold dust to build and stock a saloon.

The town was called Badger Crossing by most, simply because a man named Ike Hillman had once seen a badger fording the river, simply to get to the other side. Stinky liked the story; he always claimed that the badger was trying to get to his saloon. The sad little town still had no official name, which didn't seem to bother its three or four dozen permanent residents.

'Back from the far country, I see,' Stinky said, patting Cougar's shoulder, which he had to stretch to reach. 'How'd it go?'

'Good and bad, like most things,' Cougar replied.

'I know what you mean. How about a beer, Cougar — I've got a new recipe I've been using.'

'Did that make it better?' Cougar asked.

'It made it . . . different,' Stinky said with a laugh. 'Give it a try?'

'Why not — it's a dry day.'

Stinky slipped behind the bar, and drew a beer himself. Bringing the mug to Cougar, he asked, 'What brings you by, Cougar?'

'Business. Do you remember that money I left with you a long while back?'

'Of course I remember,' Stinky said. 'I thought you were the one who'd forgotten about it.'

'I almost had, but I've a use for it now.'

'I'll get it out for you. Too bad we don't have a bank you could have put it in, Cougar; you might have accrued a nice amount of interest by now.'

'Yes, and it's too bad we don't have strawberries and ice cream,' Cougar said. Stinky laughed. Cougar sipped at the beer, which seemed the same as Stinky's old recipe — green and tasting somehow of sawdust. He said, 'I won't worry about any interest I might have made, so long as the money hasn't dwindled on its own.'

Stinky appeared offended. 'I told you it was in my strongbox, Cougar. No one ever touches that but me.'

'All right, I apologize. Get it for me in a minute, will you?' Looking briefly around the dark saloon again, he asked the saloon owner, 'I'm looking for a man named Earl Normand — have you seen him?'

Stinky's eyes narrowed. In a lower voice he answered, 'You mean the man who took over the old Fenner place?'

'That's the one.'

'Isn't that trouble all over with?'

'That's what I want to find Normand to ask,' Cougar said, placing his mug down, half of the green beer still in it.

'He was in earlier,' Stinky said. 'Drank a beer, said he had some business to take care of and left.'

'Have you any idea of where he might have gone?'

'To Joe Compton's place, I think. His business had something to do with horses, he said.'

'Fine. I was heading over that way myself,' Cougar half-smiled, 'as soon as I have some working money in my pocket.'

'I'll get that for you right away, Cougar. I can see you're not in a patient mood,' Stinky said, a little nervously as if he did not like seeing Carroll Cougar in an impatient mood, which was probably so.

In minutes the little man was back. Cougar had spent the time looking over the new faces of Badger Crossing, which were much the same as the old ones. Travelling men going nowhere, wastrels, would-be tough guys. Cougar knew none of them and didn't care to. For the moment liquor had equalized them; the following morning would set them all apart from each other once again. But they would be the same to themselves. It was a sad little town.

As Cougar roughly counted his money and stuffed it into his pockets, Stinky asked one more question.

'Cougar, you didn't happen to get yourself married, did you?'

'I did, as a matter of fact,' Carroll Cougar replied. 'Why?'

Stinky's already distressed expression darkened. 'Because a man came in here a few hours ago and said that a woman who gave her name as Cougar had gotten herself into some trouble down at the foot of town.'

Stinky might have said more, but Cougar was paying no attention. He was heading out the door, his heart thudding, his rifle gripped tightly in his hand.

10

It was an effort of self-control not to mount his horse and race toward the other end of town, but Cougar knew that whatever had happened was already over and done, and so rigidly, his face grimly set, he led the gray that way. He needed more information before he could act. Primarily he wanted to know if Ellen was all right. Secondarily, what sort of trouble had she gotten into and who had caused it? He knew Ellen well enough to know that she could not have provoked any sort of disturbance. Therefore . . .

He was passing Joe Compton's stable when a familiar voice called out, 'Hey, Cougar!' and he turned that way to see Joe himself standing in the open double doors, a rake in his hand. Cougar paused in his headlong rush, knowing that Joe, one of the last business owners on this end of town, might have seen something. It was more sensible to ask someone who might know what had happened than to continue on blindly like an enraged bull.

'Hello, Joe,' Cougar said, aware that his face was now perspiring heavily. His hands were sweating; his knees did not feel to be solidly in place. 'I'll want to talk to you later, but something important's come up.'

Joe Compton, who was lanky, dark and affable, grinned. 'I guess you mean that business with your wife,' he said unexpectedly. He waved a dismissive hand. 'That's all over, Cougar.'

'You know about it?' Cougar asked.

'I saw it all,' Compton answered. He was still smiling. 'You should have been here!'

'I wish I had been.'

'Yes,' Compton said, frowning briefly. 'I guess you do, but it's best that you weren't; Lord knows what you would have done.'

'Tell me, Joe, and make it quick and

simple.' Cougar wanted no long-winded embellishments of the tale. He only wanted to know, needed to know, what had happened to Ellen.

'Well, she was riding a little spotted red roan, wasn't she?' Joe asked for confirmation. Cougar nodded. 'It was just about in front of me that I saw this man step in front of her horse and tell her to step down because he had some business he wanted to discuss with her. I think he was drunk, but that makes no difference. Even in Badger Crossing a man should know better than to trouble a woman.'

Cougar gritted his teeth. It was seldom you could expect a western man to get directly to the point of a good story. That might be fine for entertainment in a saloon, but Cougar needed to know what had happened and how Ellen was. He waited for what seemed like long minutes before a chuckling Joe Compton continued.

'Well, the lady says to this man, 'Mr., my name is Ellen Cougar, if that name

166

means anything to you,' and the man, he answers, 'It don't mean nothing to me; I've still got some business I want to conduct with you if you'll step down from your pony.' He was holding the bridle to the roan by now.' Joe chuckled again.

''What kind of business?' the lady asks as calm as you please. 'If you'd like to purchase a new Winchester, I've got one right here. Or maybe you'd just like a few samples from it.' That's when I knew she was surely your wife, Cougar. Had to be. She had that spanking new Winchester out of its scabbard and pointed at that street thug's brisket and he took to his heels, right enough, scared out of his wits.'

Cougar felt himself calming. 'Well, as long as she's all right — tell me, Joe, did you know the man?'

'I can't say I recognized him. He was no long-time resident,' Joe Compton replied. 'You know how people come and go around here, though.'

'That one had better just keep on

going,' Cougar said darkly.

'Well, if he didn't know your name, he hasn't been around long,' Compton said. 'Just a drunken trail bum, I'd suppose.'

'I suppose,' Cougar muttered. He was more relaxed now and he returned to other business. 'I want to talk horses, Joe, but first I want to ask you what you know about a man named Earl Normand.'

'Quite a bit, I suppose, but why don't you ask him yourself, Cougar. He's right out back, looking at a black mare he wants to buy for his niece.'

'What kind of mood is he in?' Cougar asked cautiously.

'Mister Normand? Why, he's in a fine mood. He usually is. Why do you ask, Cougar?'

'I don't know. It hasn't been a good day.' Cougar heard a scrabbling sound in the huge wooden oat bin to his left. Joe glanced that way as well and then smiled.

'I didn't think there were any of those

grain mice left in the place — haven't seen one for three months. I suppose there's always a straggler.'

'I suppose,' Cougar mumbled in response. Just then his mind was not on mice.

He decided against taking his rifle along with him. It wasn't very neighborly. But he walked out into the cool sunshine of the back yard and saw a small, florid man stroking the sleek muzzle of a young black mare. Earl Normand didn't turn his head as Cougar approached, but he asked him: 'Do you think a young woman would like this mare?'

'I don't see why not,' Cougar answered, leaning on the corral post beside Normand. 'She's a nice-looking piece of horseflesh.'

'Docile, too,' Normand replied, his attention still on the horse. 'It has fine lines. Yes, I think I will take this black home with me.'

'I'm sure Gloria will be pleased with it,' Cougar said. At this unexpected remark, the man turned his eyes toward Cougar for the first time.

'You know my niece?'

'Actually I met her for the first time this morning. My name is Carroll Cougar. I'm your neighbor from over on Twin Creek.'

'You don't say!' the affable little man said, thrusting out a pudgy hand which Cougar took. 'I understood that the place had been abandoned; well, welcome back. Was there a reason you rode over this morning?'

'I just wanted to say hello and let you people know that I was back.'

'Well, I'm glad you came by — sorry I wasn't there to greet you. Carroll Cougar — yes, I know the name. Aren't you the man who bought the property from my nephew?' There was the slightest of frowns on the round little man's face.

'That's right; I am.'

'Are you married, Mr. Cougar?'

'Yes, I am,' Cougar said, uncertain of the reason behind the question.

'Then you and your wife will have to come by some evening for supper, or perhaps just for tea in the middle of the day — anytime at all. I'm sure Gloria would be pleased at the opportunity to visit with another woman — there are so few around Badger Crossing.' The little man continued to smile, splitting his attention between Cougar and the sleek black mare.

'May I be frank with you, Mr. Normand?' Cougar asked.

'Why, of course,' the jovial little man answered.

'The reason I rode over to your ranch this morning, the reason I'm talking to you now, is that I'm trying to find out if you might be sheltering a grudge against me.'

Normand's look was one of astonishment, and Cougar was sure that it was genuine. 'Why, of course not! What possible reason could I have, Mr. Cougar?'

'Trent Fenner, your nephew, certainly did hold a grudge against me.

171

Who knows what he might have told his family.'

'Trent Fenner,' Normand said, wagging his head, 'was a delusional man — also he was not a very nice person. I hate to speak ill of the dead, especially about my own sister's son, but Trent was not a normal man.

'Mr. Cougar, I have examined the records of your deed as a precaution once I knew that Trent's ranch had been left to me. I have talked to people around Badger Crossing about you. They agree that you are a little rough around the edges, but a basically honest man. Scrupulously so, it seems. Yes, I have heard of Trent Fenner's claim that you bilked him out of the Twin Creek property, but the evidence does not back up that assertion.

'I am content now with what I have. The ranch runs fewer cattle, but we can live comfortably off it. The property was an unexpected windfall, and I am happy to have it, but we need no more — and I certainly do not wish to feud with my closest neighbor.'

The thing was, Cougar believed every word the cheerful little man was saying. He had already decided that he was probably looking in the wrong place for his sniper. There was something even more personal behind the ambush at his house. But what?

'Was that all, Mr. Cougar?' Normand asked, almost hopefully. Cougar had not moved from the rail of the corral.

'I need some horses myself,' Cougar answered. 'A stallion and a couple of mares. I don't see what I'm looking for here . . . unless you wanted to sell me that black mare.'

Normand chuckled. 'No, I think not. She was the best I saw in the herd, and as I told you, I have already determined to make a gift of it to Gloria — it hasn't been easy for a young woman, uprooting herself from her mother's house and traveling west with me to end up in what must seem to her to be the end of the world.'

'I suppose not,' Cougar said. 'I'll talk

to Joe and see if he has any recommendations for me.'

'And with that, Mr. Cougar, I will bid you a farewell, I need to lead this mare home, and she might not be all that willing to relocate. Don't forget that you have an open invitation — you and your wife — to my house.'

'I'm sure we'll be by,' Cougar said, 'though I can't say when. We're pretty busy trying to get everything back in shape.'

Joe Compton had a worried look as Cougar met him again in the stable. 'He's a nice little guy, that Earl Normand, don't you think, Cougar?'

'He seems to be.'

Joe Compton's expression relaxed. He smiled. 'The way you came in here, I didn't know what to expect.'

'I was looking for a man; now I don't think Normand was him.'

And, Cougar had already been very upset by the incident between Ellen and some local street bum when he had arrived. He was still edgy over the ambush attempt. Cougar needed to find a target to lash out against, but he was finding nothing but shadows and smoke, and those he could not fight.

The sun was beginning to lower its head when Cougar and Joe Compton again returned to the stable. Joe had showed him two fine-looking mares of the right age for foaling, and a strapping, recalcitrant, three-year-old sorrel stallion, feisty as he should be. Cougar purchased the three horses on the spot. There was time to worry about hand-taming the proud young stallion later.

'You're getting the better of me on the price,' Joe Compton said as they went into his office.

'Joe, no one's ever gotten the better of you in a horse trade,' Cougar said, telling the truth. Compton smiled despite himself.

'I try not to let them. How else could I make a living? Is this going to be a cash transaction, Cougar? Or . . . ?'

'Cash. I've been putting some money

together just for this. Have you got a few capable men who can be hired to drive them out to Twin Creek?'

'Yes, I can have that done for you, if you like. Max Stroh — oh, that's right, you wouldn't know him — and his brother. They're good with horses. I think Max was a wrangler down in Clovis before he broke his leg. His boss couldn't wait for him to heal up, and so he cut Max loose.'

'Tough,' Cougar said, sympathizing with the unknown cowhand.

'First thing in the morning, then, Cougar,' Joe said, handing Cougar the titles to the three horses. Joe smiled faintly. 'While the boys are still sober.'

Cougar gave Joe a sharp look — he could not risk losing these horses. Joe said soothingly, 'I'll let Max know tonight that I have a job for him; that'll slow him down. I guarantee the work, Cougar.'

'All right; you know them better than I do. I'll take you at your word.'

They walked out of the office then,

Cougar collecting the reins to his gray horse. Again he heard a faint scrabbling in the huge grain bin followed by a muffled, plaintive sound. Joe had been watching Cougar.

'Is there something else I can do for you?' Joe Compton asked.

'Yes, I think so. One more small thing.'

★   ★   ★

Cougar returned home in the sundown light. He continued to search the land around him with his eyes.

He was not convinced that the ambusher had simply given up and gone away. Such men do not once they have their minds set on the job.

Would the sniper wait for daylight to obtain a better target or would he just strike at any given opportunity? There was no telling.

There was chicken frying in the house; Cougar could smell it long before he reached the corral. God bless

Ellen! He himself had forgotten to purchase even a few rough provisions after the business with Stinky, with Joe Compton, with Earl Normand. There were a few burlap sacks scattered around in the shed when Cougar toted his saddle and gear there after turning the gray horse into the paddock, and Cougar felt sure that Ellen had purchased more than a chicken for them to survive on.

I should have gone with her, Cougar was thinking as he walked toward the house, saddle-bags over his shoulder. He could have helped her carry more provisions home, and that encounter in the street with the roughneck would not have happened had Cougar been there. His idea to take a ride to the Fenner place had been a dud. There was no way Cougar could see Normand in the role of a lurking sniper. He would issue no apology to Ellen but hope for forgiveness all the same.

Carroll Cougar still had not gotten the hang of this marriage business. It would take a while — most good things did.

Right now he couldn't have felt much happier about having a real home and a waiting wife. The smell of cooking as he stepped into the cabin was tantalizing, reassuring and comforting at once. Ellen was in the kitchen doorway. Too late she tried to warn him.

'Carroll, watch out for' — and then Cougar stumbled over some unknown object and tumbled heavily to the floor — 'the dog,' Ellen finished. She had gone to where Cougar lay. On the floor beside him, licking at his face in apology was a yellow mongrel pup with huge, awkward-looking paws, sagging jowls and ears which drooped to the floor. It couldn't have been more than four or five months old. As Cougar rose to his feet, the little dog began to roll around and wriggle against the floor. There was a spreading wet spot under its belly.

The yellow pup halted, sat and looked up at Cougar with expressive brown eyes and then began the entire ritual of apology over again.

'He's saying he's sorry for making you trip,' Ellen said, crouching to scratch the loose hide on the dog's skull.

'I understood that much,' Cougar answered. 'How long do *I* have to apologize for nearly stepping on him?'

Cougar stood looking down at the ungainly yellow pup before smiling and turning his head away. Maybe it would calm down if it no longer thought it was the center of attention. Cougar walked to Ellen, kissed her and said: 'You know that this is the ugliest-looking pup I've ever seen in my life.'

'Is it not?' she replied. 'No one would ever love him just for being cute. That's why I brought him home; what else could I do?'

'Left him where he was.'

'He was at the store where I went. Oh, Cougar, they didn't want him. I saw one of the men aim a kick at him. I don't know what they would have done to him eventually — whatever it is that they do with unwanted pups. I had to bring him home.'

'It's all right, but . . . '

Ellen had suddenly become aware of a wriggling presence in Cougar's saddle-bags. A pathetic little cry accompanied this movement. Ellen's eyes widened a little, questioning.

Cougar unbuckled his saddle-bag flap. As he did he said, 'You know I detest rats, Ellen. Well, we have at least one in the house. While I was at Joe Compton's stable he told me about the problem they used to have with mice in their grain bin. Joe somehow came by a pair of cats a few months ago, and they've pretty much solved the problem for him. So I thought . . . '

Cougar had a coal-black kitten by the scruff, and now he pulled it from his saddle-bags and held it for Ellen to see. She took it and held it more gently, scratching the cat's ears. It was fluffy and dark, probably ninety percent fur and ten percent cat.

'Cougar, the rats I have seen are bigger than he is!'

'Well,' Cougar said with a sheepish smile, 'it's sure to grow.'

'Yes, that's true.'

'The thing is, I didn't know we had a dog — how could I? They don't mix well, you know.'

'Oh, Cougar — they're both still babies. It'll be fine.'

It seemed so. By the time they had eaten their chicken dinner and readied for bed, the pup was stretched out on its back, huge paws in the air, asleep, and the tiny black kitten was curled up on one of the yellow dog's broad ears, twitching and mewling with apparent pleasure.

Cougar stood with his arm around Ellen's slender shoulders. She looked up and smiled.

'That does make it seem more like home, doesn't it? I guess we were both right in doing what we did.'

'It looks like it. What do you say we get to bed? Today was a long day, and tomorrow doesn't promise to be much easier. There's work to be done, and I told you Stinky is sending our three new horses out.'

As they started down the hallway toward the bedroom, Ellen halted unexpectedly and turned to face Cougar.

'Have you ever seen Calvin D'Arcy with a beard, Carroll?'

'D'Arcy?' Cougar answered blankly. 'No, why would you ask me that?'

'It's just that the man who accosted me today had a full beard, but underneath it it seemed I recognized someone I knew.'

'Calvin D'Arcy is miles away,' Cougar believed. 'Besides, why would he choose to approach you that way? Has he even had the time to grow a beard? It seems unlikely. No, it seems you are trying too hard to find a solution to all of our problems, Ellen. As am I. Tracking down Earl Normand was futile.'

'It's just that for a moment there in town . . . oh, I don't know, Carroll, you must be right.'

'There's also the fact that you told the man your name and he had never heard it before.'

'Or claimed not to,' Ellen said. 'There is a difference.'

'Yes. Yes, there is,' Cougar said thoughtfully. Still the suspicion carried no weight. There was no sense to it, really. Calvin D'Arcy of all people would have known that there was nothing he could have done that would provoke Cougar more.

Unless provoking Cougar had been his intention . . .

'Come on, Ellen, we both need a good night's sleep. Our brains are running in circles, getting nowhere.'

★ ★ ★

Settling in bed with the silver moon shining through the high window of their bedroom, Cougar had his arm around Ellen, who was already asleep. Cougar had not been able to still his own speculations. No matter how drunk the man who had molested Ellen had been, he must have known that, as Joe Compton said, even in a town like Badger Crossing the men would not stand for such a thing.

So he had not been local. Had he even been a Western man? Anyone from this part of the country would know that he was breaking a taboo. So perhaps he was not a Westerner at all. He was bearded, Ellen said. And he was someone who did not know Cougar's name in a territory where most men who had never even met him knew him by reputation.

The stranger had said that he wanted to discuss business with Ellen. Was that just a ruse, or had he actually believed that there was business between them? What sort of business?

Cougar lay staring at the ceiling while Ellen slept softly. Ignoring his own good advice, Cougar's own mind still whirred with the problem. He needed to find a cause behind it all before he could put an end to it.

Just then he was focused on the man in the street — not a Western man. Bearded. Someone Ellen thought she had seen before. One with business to conduct with her.

Dammit, that led him back in a crazy circle to the Brotherhood, many of whom had followed Ellen and her father from the east, seeking to recover money misappropriated from the church. The ones Cougar had met — Matthew and his friends — had all been bearded. Ellen could have recognized the unknown man, someone she knew only slightly from there. And he would have business he wanted to discuss if he believed that Ellen still had the stolen church funds. Also, he might not have learned Cougar's name, coming from where he did.

Cougar turned over in bed, tired of the circular patterns his mind had been travelling lately. It seemed there was no end to it. Or maybe he was just too simple-minded to solve something which was as simple as a Chinese wooden puzzle — once you knew the secret to it. He had to get some sleep, he knew. He yawned, stretched and threw his arm over his face.

Ten minutes later the bullets began to rain down against the roof of the house.

11

It was a single rifle that was being fired at the house; Cougar knew that by the spacing of the shots. Ellen awoke as Cougar moved, concerned but not cowering as she sat up in her nightdress.

'What is it, Carroll?' she asked, her voice quavering just a little.

'Our friend's come back,' Cougar said, stepping into his trousers. Just as he said that a bullet splatted against the roof of the house followed by the loud, close report of a rifle.

'Why? What does he . . . ?' She began scrambling from bed herself as Cougar stamped into his boots and grabbed his Spencer. 'What are you going to do?'

'I'm going out after him, of course,' Cougar told his wife. 'I won't have this.'

'But how can you hope to — ?'

'I don't know,' Cougar said honestly,

'but I've been in worse positions, Ellen.'

'I know, but . . . ' Ellen hurried along the hallway after him, her feet bare. There was enough moonlight to see that the yellow pup was scurrying across the floor on its belly, eyes wide with fright.

The kitten was nowhere to be seen. Presumably it had rushed under the sofa to hide.

'They don't deserve this,' Ellen said, sitting to hold the pup. 'We tried to bring them to a place of safety.'

'We don't deserve it either, Ellen,' Cougar said, starting to put his hat on before changing his mind and leaving it on the rack beside the door. 'This might take me awhile. Get the Winchester down if it makes you feel safer.'

Then Cougar was gone, slipping out the back door off the kitchen, feeling that it would probably be a safer exit from the house. The silver moon was dying in the west, offering little in the way of illumination, but Cougar knew his way in the darkness. He sprinted toward the shelter of the woodpile behind the barn, drawing no searching fire from the rifleman.

Pausing there for a minute, Cougar scoured the dark land with his senses, seeing nothing, hearing not a sound. The sniper had the advantage of having chosen his position, and he was shielded by the cloak of darkness.

But he was not safe from the prowling cougar.

Gathering himself, Cougar slipped into the thin grove of cottonwood trees that sheltered the barn. Again there was no pursuing shot as Cougar wound through the shadows cast by the slender trees. His boots made only faint whispering sounds over the earth despite his size. He was a man used to moving silently and quickly. It was a deadly haste that moved him forward, wraithlike. Pausing beside a tree, Cougar again let his eyes search the area. He was at a definite disadvantage. He did not know the sniper's position. There had been no muzzle flash, no gun-smoke since he had slipped out of the house to mark the man's position, whereas unless the ambusher was blind he must have seen Cougar rushing through the trees.

Cougar briefly revealed himself deliberately, and again no shot was fired his way. Cougar was puzzled — this was not the sort of enemy he was used to facing. He began again after taking a deep, slow breath. It got on his nerves — no man likes to be a target without a chance of fighting back, but it was not the first time for him. Eventually the other man would show himself, had to if he was going to make a fight of it.

Half an hour on Cougar found a part of what he was looking for — a small part. By following the sight line to a low ridge which offered the best field of fire for the sniper, he moved through the dull moonlight until he came upon it.

It was little enough, only the fresh sign of a horse's spoor. Of the horse, there was no sign, of its rider nothing at all. There were no hoof prints that Cougar could make out in the poor light, no other sign of activity on the ridge, although there should have been. There should have been brass cartridge casings from the sniper's rifle to mark his position.

These had apparently been carefully gathered which gave Cougar pause to consider. The would-be killer seemed to be more concerned with hiding, concealing his identity than finishing the job he had set out to do. It was an unusual consideration in Cougar's experience.

Unless his real intention was only to drive Cougar and Ellen away and not to actually kill them. That was something new to think about. And it could not be counted on. The sniper might grow frustrated if his plan did not work and decide that there was only one way to handle matters.

The enemy's battle plan was unclear and so Cougar's counterplan could not be formulated. He was still fighting smoke and shadows, and he did not like the feeling.

The sun had been up for an hour only when Max Stroh and his nameless brother appeared in Cougar's yard. They had the two mares following them on loose tethers, but each man held a lasso looped around the neck of the strapping, willful stallion between them.

The fractious sorrel shook his head wildly, trying to throw off the restraining ropes. It backed away and reared up on its hind legs. Max Stroh, for that was who Cougar took the older man of the pair to be, asked, 'Want us to try to get them all into the corral?'

The corral was already occupied by Cougar's gray and Ellen's little sorrel. They watched the new arrivals with interest, and Cougar thought with some trepidation where the sorrel was concerned.

'No, I want them turned out to pasture — I'll show you the way.'

'That's a relief,' the younger Stroh said, removing his hat to wipe his brow.

Both men were perspiring despite the cool of the morning. 'I'd rather just cut him loose than make him go somewhere he doesn't want to be.'

'He's a devil, all right,' Max Stroh agreed. 'He was fighting us all the way.'

'Are you going to try to throw a saddle over that horse?' his brother asked.

'Not at present, no,' Cougar replied. The younger Stroh looked vaguely disappointed.

'Too bad. I'd pay to watch a man trying to bust that bronco.'

Ellen had approached them. She stood watching the sleek, quivering stallion. She stepped nearer and lifted a hand as if to stroke that dark nose with the white blaze but the animal backed away and made a swift move with its head as if it would bite. Ellen withdrew her hand quickly.

'Well,' she said, 'he didn't actually bite me although he could have. Give him time; he'll come around.'

'About the time his teeth start to fall

out,' Max Stroh said. 'You said you'd show us where to cut him loose.'

'All three of them,' Cougar said. 'Give me a minute to get saddled and I'll take you out there.'

The Stroh brothers waited impatiently as Cougar saddled the gray. Both men appeared sober; both looked like they weren't enjoying staying that way. Cougar led the way out on to the wide back pasture where the three horses were turned loose. The two little mares looked around uneasily, unsure of where to go. They had never been in open country before. Their entire lives had been spent in pens. The sorrel stallion, on the other hand, lined out at a dead run for far places.

'You're going to lose that horse,' Max Stroh said.

'He can't get away. Besides, after we're gone he'll be wanting the company of these two little girls here. It'll take some time, but I'll calm him down. Once he finds out that nothing is required of him and there's no place to escape to, he'll be content enough. It just takes some patience on my part.'

When the Stroh brothers rode away, presumably headed for Stinky Barret's to spend their pay, Cougar returned to the ranch yard. There were half a dozen new intruders there — of the feathery kind. Ellen had a flock of chickens near her as she scattered feed from her skirt. Cougar put the gray away and returned to the porch where she sat, watching the chickens peck at the dusty ground.

'Another surprise,' Cougar said, sagging to the porch beside her.

'Well, Cougar, it shouldn't be that much of a surprise. After all, why would I buy just one chicken for your dinner?'

'You must have loaded that sorrel down pretty well yesterday.'

'I did what I could. The pantry isn't half full, though. We'll have to get into town again one of these days.' She was thoughtful for a minute, watching the chickens. 'Do you know, for all the squawking they did while we were catching them, once they were in the sack they didn't make a peep.'

'They're funny birds. I think they get so frightened they just pass out.'

'A pup will go to sleep if he thinks he's going to get in serious trouble.'

'Speaking of which, I hope you have some sort of plan to keep the dog from chasing the chickens.'

'I'll teach him,' Ellen said, getting to her feet, dusting off her skirt, 'or the rooster will.'

'These hens, they're all layers?' Cougar asked.

'They're supposed to be.' Ellen smiled crookedly. 'They'd better be. If not — I make some pretty good chicken and dumplings.'

The pup emerged from the house and made his way over to sit beside Cougar, watching the birds. That was all right — they wanted him to get used to them and not become excited when he saw one. 'I'm going back inside,' Ellen said, and as she turned to go the pup jumped up awkwardly and dashed toward the door to be with her.

Ten minutes later Cougar came to his feet as well, figuring it was time to get some work done. His move toward the tool shed was halted by the arrival of two armed men in the yard.

'Is your name Cougar?' the leaner of the two asked as Cougar started that way.

'That's right.' Cougar studied them. One thin and hatchet-faced, the other shorter with a pushed-in sort of nose. Both of them were whiskered — they had the look of long-riding men about them.

'My name's Ben Christian,' the lean man said. 'This is Lou Gillette.'

Cougar only nodded. Were the names supposed to mean something to him? They did not.

'We ride for Sulky Greaves,' Ben Christian said. Again Cougar could only nod.

'Mr. Greaves wants your land,' Christian said a little more darkly.

'He can't have it,' Cougar said coldly.

'You haven't even heard his terms,'

Christian said. 'You've got some good cattle land here going to waste.'

'I don't want to listen to Mr. Greaves's terms. As far as I'm concerned my land is being well used as it is.'

'You're making a mistake, Cougar,' the man called Gillette said.

'Could be,' Cougar allowed. 'It wouldn't be the first time in my life I've made one. If Greaves couldn't even make the effort to come and talk to me himself, he probably doesn't value the property that highly, which is fine by me. I'm not selling, will never sell. You can tell him just that, and tell him not to waste his time coming over personally. It will be a long ride for nothing.'

'I think you'd better listen,' Christian went on. Now the man's face had darkened. He let his horse take a few steps closer to Cougar.

Ellen had appeared on the porch, and the visitors glanced that way. She held Cougar's Spencer repeater in her hands. 'Do you think you'll be needing this today, Carroll?' she asked in a quiet, steady voice.

'I'm not sure yet; what do you think, boys?' he asked the two riders.

Christian and Gillette did not like the hard look in Cougar's eyes, the set of his mouth — that was obvious. Both could see Cougar's holstered Colt and both knew that Ellen could flip the big-bored rifle to Cougar easily.

'Aw, I don't think so,' Ben Christian said, waving a hand. 'We'll just have to tell Mr. Greaves that we made you the offer and you didn't accept it.'

'Will that be the end of it?' Cougar asked as the men turned their horses' heads away.

'I couldn't say, Cougar, we're just the messenger boys. What Sulky Greaves might decide, I couldn't guess.'

Ellen came to stand beside Cougar as the two riders left, trailing dust. 'What was that about?' she asked, taking Cougar's arm.

'Some man I never heard of, a Mr. Sulky Greaves, wants our land.'

'Oh, Cougar,' Ellen said with a heartfelt sigh. 'Is there anybody who doesn't want our land?'

'Things could be worse,' Cougar thought. 'Someone could have just taken it over while I was gone. Then I'd have to figure out a way to get them off it again.'

'Maybe that's it!' Ellen said. The pup had followed her out and down the steps and now had a good hold on her shirt hem. She bent and shooed it away. 'I mean, you were gone a long time out on the desert with General Crook. Maybe the word got around that there was an abandoned piece of land here with good graze and plentiful water.'

'Could be, I suppose,' Cougar said thoughtfully. 'I couldn't blame a man like Greaves for asking about it. It's the way it was done that I didn't like.'

'There's something else you don't like about it,' Ellen said, knowing her husband.

'Yes, there is. Our list of potential enemies has grown again. About the

201

only person I don't suspect these days is Stinky Barret — and I'm not too sure about him!' Cougar laughed.

'You'd better get to work,' Ellen said, rubbing his back in a circular motion. 'Maybe it will get your mind off things. What did you have planned for today?'

'I thought I'd better clean out the old well so we don't have to walk to the creek for water. I'm still going to have to dig a new one when I have the time, when everything is settled, but I'll need some help with that project. That's for later, probably not today,' Cougar said, lifting his eyes. 'I'm going to have to get up on that roof and see what sort of shape it's in. I don't have the lumber to firm the porch up yet, so I'll let that go. I could break out some whitewash for the corral posts — '

Ellen interrupted him. 'Carroll, stop. We both know there's still a lot to do. Pick one job — any job — and start on that one.'

Cougar nodded his head. 'The old well, then.'

'Good,' Ellen said. She asked again, 'Do you want to take your rifle with you?'

'The way things are — yes, I suppose I'd better carry it along with me.'

The old well was on the far side of the barn. There were planks over the well, and underneath a ten-foot-deep framework meant to prevent cave-ins. This had not done the job well. Mud had accumulated along with various sorts of green slime. It was no longer a well, but only a breeding place for mosquitoes. A bucket and rope would be required for clean-up before Cougar could even see the borehole beneath the muck.

It was a filthy job, and the kind Cougar hated, but it was his fault for not maintaining the well properly. After shifting the covering planks from the well he went to the barn and found a good length of rope and a five-gallon bucket which should suit his purpose. He also found a shovel in the corner. When had he left that there? It belonged in the tool shed.

He had nearly returned to the well when he sensed, then saw the approaching rider on the ridge to the south. The horse he recognized almost immediately; he had been looking at the little black mare just yesterday. Riding it was Gloria Fenner. Cougar dropped his tools and placed his rifle aside to greet the woman, who was wearing a forest-green riding habit and a dark hat.

'Hello, Miss Fenner,' he said, greeting the incoming rider. 'Taking the mare out for a try?'

'Yes, she's such an easy creature to ride — very soft-footed. I started to just ride across your valley, but I saw a new horse out there and he was acting a little wild — a big sorrel stallion.'

'Yes, he was just delivered and he is a little on the wild side. You made the right decision detouring around him.'

Cougar was stroking the placid little mare's nose. The horse had not been ridden hard or far, and seemed content with its new lot in life.

'Is your wife at home, Mr. Cougar? Uncle Earl told me that you were married.'

'She's in the house, working; there's still a lot of cleaning-up to do around here.'

'Maybe I can convince her to take a little time away from her chores to sit and visit with me — I want to meet her.'

'I'm sure she'd be happy to visit with you, Miss Fenner. May I take your horse and water it for you?'

'I'd appreciate that,' Gloria Fenner said. The woman spoke all the right words, Cougar thought, but her face was still tight and those slate-gray eyes of hers refused to smile. With Cougar holding the black mare's bridle, Gloria Fenner swung down and walked toward the house. She still carried her riding crop, Cougar noticed.

'Come on, Little Bit,' Cougar said to the black mare, 'let's find you some water.'

By the time Cougar returned from

watering the mare at the creek, Gloria still had not emerged from the house. He left the black horse tied at the hitching rail and got back to the well. It was an hour or so later, while Cougar stood calf-deep in sludge and mud with his shovel, making slow, dirty progress through the ooze, that Gloria reappeared. She climbed aboard the little black mare and rode out again the way she had come. She waved a hand to Cougar and offered him a meaningless smile as she passed.

At noon Ellen came out to remind Cougar that it was time for lunch. She found him, muddy to his knees, looking down into the well with a small smile. She walked beside him and saw the clear water piping its way up from the depths of the well.

Cougar put his arm around his woman's waist. 'Funny how such a small triumph can cheer a man up,' he said.

'Yes,' Ellen agreed.

'The trouble around here right now,

is that the end of any job is just a reminder that there are a dozen left to be done.'

'They tell me that's the way life works,' Ellen said as they started back toward the house.

'I know it. The trouble is that I spent so many years as a fighting man that I'm more used to things that have a more definite beginning and ending. We charged the enemy and we won or we lost. It was ended. Nothing continued endlessly.'

'Except Carlina,' Ellen said without looking at Cougar.

'Why would you bring her up?' Cougar asked.

'Because I wonder sometimes how much of her lingers around you. This is the house you built for her, isn't it?'

Cougar took a deep breath, halted her and lifted her chin with his thumb. 'No,' he said honestly. 'This is the home I built for myself. Now it is yours. *Ours*. I don't want to hear that kind of talk ever again.'

'All right, Cougar. I promise. A woman gets funny ideas sometimes, as you know.'

'Speaking of which,' Cougar said as they started on, now accompanied by the yellow pup, which had gotten out somehow, 'what do you think of our new neighbor?'

'Gloria? She was nice enough — in a quite formal way. It was as if she was paying a visit only out of duty, though why she should feel she had that obligation, I couldn't say.'

'And?'

'And what? I don't know, Carroll, I just didn't feel comfortable with her around. She looked around the house like a robber planning a bank job. What do they call it, 'casing' the place?'

Cougar laughed. 'There isn't a whole lot in our vault, Ellen.'

'Oh, I didn't mean it literally. There was just something furtive about her I didn't care for. Have you seen her eyes?'

'Yes, I have,' Cougar replied. 'There

isn't a lot of life or kindness in them.'

'Or any other emotion. You can tell that she's always thinking, but she gives no indication of what it might be. Cougar, I plain don't trust that woman.'

12

After lunch, Cougar returned to the well. Clear water was still rising freely and he began to try to convince himself that he did not need to dig a new well after all. Replacing the planks covering it, he returned his tools to their proper places. He spent a little time tending to and visiting with the two horses in the corral. Both the gray and the roan seemed content to waste the day away.

There was still a good chunk of the day left, and Cougar himself could not waste it. He considered looking at the roof to see what needed to be done up there, then settled for the easier job of applying whitewash to every bit of bare wood in sight — the corral posts, the porch uprights and rails. Three hours later he was not so sure he had chosen the easier job. His back ached from bending and stooping; he was spattered with whitewash, his jeans were still heavy with mud, now dry and caked. He must have looked as if he'd just risen from the grave.

He looked up from the nearly empty pail and noticed a few places that he had missed that he should not have and realized that it was at least partially due to the fading sunlight. He immediately convinced himself that since he could not see well enough to do the job right, it was time to quit. His body was ready to give it up anyway.

He stood, dropped the brush into the pail and stretched to try easing a crick in his back.

It was then that he saw Calvin D'Arcy crossing the yard on a paint pony, riding slowly toward the house. Cougar dropped the bucket he had been holding in his right hand and let his fingers linger near his holstered revolver.

'You look like hell, Cougar,' the army scout said, reaching the porch. He glanced around at the house, the yard.

'Seems like you're making progress here, though.'

'What do you want here, Calvin?'

'Not much. Do you mind if I swing down? I've been in leather for most of the day.'

'Just stay on this side of your horse,' Cougar said. D'Arcy nodded and dismounted.

'I see you haven't forgotten that time in Clovis when I fouled up that highwayman's plans,' D'Arcy commented. On that occasion the would-be robber ordered D'Arcy and a man named MacMillan to dismount, but D'Arcy had fooled the man by swinging down on the wrong side of his horse, gaining protection for himself. D'Arcy had shot the robber dead across the saddle.

'I haven't forgotten much where it comes to you,' Cougar said tightly.

'That's what I figured. That's why I'm here, Cougar.'

The front door had opened and from the corner of his eye, Cougar saw Ellen emerge. 'Will you be much longer, Carroll . . . ?' Then she recognized Calvin D'Arcy. 'Oh!' she said. It was a breathy, unhappy exhalation.

'Hello, Ellen,' D'Arcy said.

'Will you be having supper with us?' Ellen asked, her voice still unsteady.

'I don't know where I'll be going, if anywhere. That's what I've come to ask Cougar.'

'I don't understand you, Calvin,' Cougar said.

'It's kind of private, Cougar,' D'Arcy said, looking at Ellen, who took her cue and with a last worried look at the two men returned to the house, clumsy pup galumphing after her.

'All right, Calvin, let's get down to it. Why are you here?'

'I kept thinking, Cougar, about the way you had tracked other men down — Solon Reineke for example — and I got up every day not knowing if that would be the day you came after me. I just couldn't live that way anymore. I had to come back here to see where

213

things stood between us. If you wanted me dead.'

Cougar remained silent for a long minute. His eyes were raised to the western sky which was coloring now as dusk set in. Finally he spoke.

'There was a moment in time when I thought I'd rise from my bed and kill you, Calvin. But I got to thinking about all the trails we traveled together, all the campfires and meals we shared. Also, I didn't see how what happened with Carlina could be all your fault.

'Mostly,' he said, nodding toward the house where kitchen sounds were audible, 'there's Ellen. I'd kill to protect her, to avenge her, but I'm not going to go out on the prowling trail and maybe get killed myself for the sake of an old injury. My job is to stay with her and protect her, not to ramble around like a crazy man, carrying hatred in his heart. I've done that, Calvin, and it was not very satisfying as a way of life.'

'Then it's over?' Calvin D'Arcy asked.

'It's over as far as I'm concerned. But, Calvin — would you do us both a favor and just ride out of here? I don't need any reminders of the past. Not here, not anymore.'

'All right, Cougar. I guess I can understand that. I just had to know, you understand?'

'I understand. Excuse me if I never wish to see you again.'

Calvin D'Arcy mounted and turned his horse into the sunset, vanishing into the darkness. Cougar tramped back into the house. Ellen was in the kitchen. She turned from the stove to look at him.

'Calvin won't be staying for supper?'

'No. He had to go,' Cougar replied.

There were questions lingering in Ellen's eyes, but none were spoken. 'What did you manage to whip up?' Cougar wondered, knowing how low their supplies were.

'How's ham and eggs sound?'

'Fine by me. You managed to bring that back too?'

'Yes. It's not that I'm that resourceful, Cougar — it's just that I didn't wish to go hungry!'

'We'll remedy that. We will get back into Badger Crossing and bring home a stock of supplies — if I have to rent a wagon to do it.'

When Cougar had washed up and seated himself at the table, he was served. A nicely fried slice of country ham was on his platter. A single fried egg was its companion. He frowned slightly with his eyebrows.

'You don't get many eggs in a sack these days, I suppose,' Cougar said.

He looked across the table at Ellen, who was smiling for some reason. He noticed that she had two eggs on her plate. 'All right, what is it?' he asked.

'I gave you the special egg,' she said proudly. 'It was the only one.'

'Special?' It looked to Cougar like any other egg he had seen.

'My eggs,' Ellen explained, 'the others on the counter — those are all store-bought eggs. Yours,' she announced happily,

216

'was laid by one of our very own hens today.'

Cougar smiled. 'In that case, I'm sure it will taste better than any of the others.'

'I'm sure it will,' Ellen answered, and he was not sure if she was joking or not. When he cut it and took a bite, he could swear himself that there was something special about the way that particular egg tasted.

It was a quiet, peaceful evening in front of the fire. The pup was asleep on Ellen's feet. The black kitten which had re-emerged from its hiding place had clawed its way up on to the couch where it kneaded Cougar's lap for a while — something it could be trained out of later, but not tonight, its second in its new home. Finished with that maneuver, it settled down with only it's fuzzy head on Cougar's leg. Ellen was knitting. She had planned ahead for nights like this; she had had a busy day shopping for this and that.

There was something soothing about

the clicking of her knitting needles, the softly burning fire. Cougar was at peace; he began to doze off.

The racketing of rifle fire brought him instantly from his doze. The cat scurried away, the pup began its fearful quivering. Cougar grabbed his rifle. Since he had used the back door the night before, he went out the front this time. He was in time to see a muzzle flash from the ridge as a bullet slammed into the house.

'Stay in the house,' he commanded.

Had D'Arcy come back? Cougar wondered, but D'Arcy was a straightforward man and no coward. He had proved that by riding up to the house earlier. Cougar was fairly certain he knew who the sniper was now. The conclusion he had drawn did not make him happy, but that made no difference. The sniper was threatening his life, his home, his wife and must be eliminated quickly and permanently.

You can't leave a rattlesnake free to slither around where it will and strike when it is so inclined.

Cougar decided against taking the direct approach this time. The marksman was unskilled as a warrior, or he would not have chosen the same position to fire from again. The sniper was also very cautious or he would not have fled as Cougar had approached the night before. So, instead of rushing directly to the ridge, Cougar decided to circle wide and come up on the high ground from behind. That would at least cut off any escape route. Or so he hoped.

He also hoped that Ellen would stay low and that no unlucky shot penetrated the walls of the house. As Cougar trekked along the grassy hillside the rifle above was fired twice more. Carefully spaced shots, they were, as if the sniper was enjoying himself, taking his time as he inflicted terror on the innocent. Carroll Cougar could not even imagine what he would do if any harm came to Ellen, if she were killed. Probably, he thought, he would go quite mad and be unfit for civilized company the rest of his life.

There had been quite enough of this sniper and his menace. It would end tonight one way or the other — Cougar would allow no more of it. The silver moon was again vague in the sky when Cougar reached a small path he knew leading to the ridge. He made his way up it as carefully, as silently as an Apache warrior.

The sporadic gunfire had stopped. Did that mean the rifleman was going to try to make his escape — or had already made it? Cougar reasoned that since he had seen no horseman pass, the sniper must still be on the ridge, and he approached the skyline carefully, his rifle already cocked and ready.

He thought as he paused once that he heard a horse moving away, but he could not even be sure in the silence of the night. New grass still sprouted there, muffling every sound of movement. He edged up over the rim, hiding himself behind a low stack of boulders.

The moonlight glinted off the face of the mica-laden rocks, but did little to illuminate the dark land. Cougar held his position for long minutes. Still he heard no sounds — nothing like the levering of a cartridge into the receiver of a Winchester, nothing like the impatient sounds of a horse shifting its feet.

Cougar took a deep breath. There was nothing to do but step out from behind the rocks. And into the rifleman's sights. But it was now that it must be done; it was now that this must be ended. Cougar emerged from his hiding place with his rifle at the ready.

He found himself standing alone on the barren ridge in the cool of night.

But he had seen no horseman pass. Where could the sniper have gone?

The answer chilled Cougar to the bone. The rifleman could have gone nowhere but directly down toward Cougar's house where Ellen waited alone. Cursing, Cougar began a scrambling descent down the grassy bluff, slipping and sliding in his haste. He seemed to have been outsmarted. The sniper had somehow noticed Cougar's approach and knew that the house was unguarded.

Cougar rushed on, his breath tight in his chest, his heart pounding, blood singing in his ears. Reaching the flat ground he pounded on recklessly toward the house.

In the night the crack of a Winchester rifle was clear and sharp.

Rushing past a standing horse in front of the house, Cougar looked toward the open door, and by the lantern light within he could see the spilled, inert figure of a woman sprawled against the floor. The little yellow pup had begun to howl pitiably.

13

'I warned her not to try it,' Ellen said, throwing herself into Cougar's arms. She was trembling badly, her legs loose under her. 'But she wouldn't listen. Is she mad?'

'I don't know. I think maybe she is,' Cougar said, looking down at the woman on the floor. Gloria Fenner's own rifle lay near her open hand, and Cougar picked it up and moved it away. Gloria was able to reach out and try to stop him. She was still alive. Ellen's shot had been a good enough one. It had slammed into Gloria's shoulder just below the collarbone. Possibly the bone had been fractured as well, but the slug from the Winchester had continued on in its inexorable path through flesh and slammed into the wall behind her.

'Well,' Cougar said, looking up, 'I guess we'd better see what we can do for her.'

'I don't care to do anything for her!' Ellen spat. 'I hope she dies.'

'I don't think you mean that,' Cougar said. Ellen shook her head and sighed.

'You're right, I don't. But, Carroll, she came into my house, our own house and threatened to kill us!'

'I know. I guess she decided that just trying to drive us off was not going to work.'

'But why, Carroll? Why was she doing it at all?' Ellen asked as she helped Cougar place the injured woman on the sofa.

'I suppose in her mind she had every reason to try to get even. I did kill her brother and her two nephews — even though they were the ones who came looking for a fight. And to her way of thinking, we were living free and easy on property which should have been a part of her inheritance.'

'But, I thought that you told me that Gloria had inherited nothing, that the Fenner property all belonged to her Uncle Earl now.'

'Yes, and that must have been another thing that irked her,' Cougar said as Ellen cut away the fabric at the shoulder of Gloria's blouse with a pair of shears. 'Earl Normand being the nearest male relative had inherited, and Normand had looked into matters and decided that Trace Fenner had been in the wrong. Gloria could not accept that conclusion. In the end all she had gotten from the settlement was a black mare. The little girl gets her pony to appease her.'

'But she had a fine place to live, a ranch which presumably would be hers one day, safety, security, comparative wealth — much more than many women have.'

'But not as much as she wanted,' Cougar said, as Ellen got to work on the bullet hole, her mouth set tightly in concentration, 'and there was the matter of revenge.'

'That emotion can run deep,' Ellen murmured.

'It always has,' Cougar said without

either of them mentioning what they were actually talking about. Yes, the impulse for revenge can run deeply enough to cause a person to forsake reason in its pursuit. No one knew that better than Carroll Cougar, who had lost many long months of his life seeking vengeance against a man who had not deserved the blame. Solon Reineke had not been responsible for Carlina's death.

It seems that if a man lives long enough he will eventually find himself on the other side of the same coin.

'What do we do with her now?' Ellen asked when she had done all she could to tend the wound with her poor supplies.

'I'll have to ride over and tell her uncle. He can take her home, and from then on it's up to him to decide what needs to be done.'

'She ought to be committed to an institution!' Ellen said, her anger returning.

'That's for Earl Normand to decide,'

Cougar said, taking Ellen into his arms again. He was considering that there were times in everyone's life when it would seem that they would be better off committed.

'I do feel terrible about having shot her,' Ellen said as they sat watching their patient. They could not afford to leave her untended. 'But she barged in here with her rifle at the ready. What else was I to do?'

'There was nothing else you could have done,' Cougar said, trying to give Ellen a little comfort. She scooted nearer to him and stroked the fluffy kitten which was purring contentedly on Cougar's lap. The fire had burned itself out, but it was not cold in the room.

'In a way,' Cougar continued, 'the woman can count herself lucky. If I'd been here I would have probably fired myself, and at this range, that .56 of mine would have torn her half apart.'

'Is that the reason you still carry that antique, Carroll?'

'I think that used to be a part of it,' he answered thoughtfully. 'A lot of it has more to do with habit. I've always carried it and so I still do even when I can hardly find ammunition for it anymore. It might be time to put the old gun away. The old days were fine, but they're gone.' He glanced at Ellen. 'We have to concentrate on what is to come, not what has gone before, don't you think?'

'Yes, I think,' Ellen said almost solemnly. There was enough heat remaining in the dead fire to color her face prettily.

She began talking about the chickens, telling Cougar that she had named every one of the hens, but was at a loss for a rooster's name. Cougar nodded comfortably and let his eyelids close. He, too, was slipping into the future and away from the past.

★ ★ ★

With dawn's first light Cougar headed out toward the Fenner ranch. He reached it just as Normand was coming out on to his porch to smoke his pipe following breakfast. He watched Cougar riding toward him, his eyes seeming to reflect knowledge of what was to come.

'Bad news, Mr. Cougar?' the little man asked. There was none of his normal cheerfulness about him this morning.

'Afraid so,' Cougar told Normand. 'Your niece has been over shooting at my house for the past few nights now. Last evening she invited herself to be shot in return.'

'Did you . . . ?'

'My wife had to, and she's feeling none too good about it.'

'No, I suppose not.' Normand tucked his pipe away in his coat pocket without having lit it. 'Is Gloria . . . ?'

'She's alive, but she needs further medical help. Whatever we could do for her was pretty crude work.'

'I should have known this would happen,' Normand said vaguely. 'I knew she had gone out riding alone at night — I thought it was just something she needed to do to feel free and to be alone. I was hoping it wasn't something like this, but I should have known.'

'How could you have?' Cougar asked, placing one boot on the lowest step.

'It seems to be in their blood — the Fenners. The children's father got himself hanged down in El Paso. They say it was just because he could not let an imagined slight go. He killed the man in front of twenty witnesses. Trace was not a normal man either — to take his own sons into a battle that caused their death was damnable. Probably he had the boys convinced that they were fighting a just fight. Trace might have believed it himself. Their brains just don't work as a normal person's does.'

Earl Normand was silent for a minute, alone with his own thoughts. Cougar felt sorry for the little man.

'Gloria's mother — my sister — asked me to bring her daughter west with me when I came. Gloria was out of hand at home. I guess we both thought a change of scenery would do her some good. We were both wrong. I sincerely thought that having a home, a fine little mare that she could ride wherever she wanted, whenever she liked would help get rid of her demons. I suppose I was naive.'

'Demons are a hard thing to banish,' Cougar said sympathetically.

'You sound like a man who has had some experience with them,' Normand said. 'Never mind responding to that — it's not my business.' He sighed. 'What should I do now, Mr. Cougar?'

'You're asking the wrong man. To institutionalize her might mean she could get some help; it might mean the end to her life as a free woman. I'm glad it's not my decision to make.'

'I suppose I could send her home, but the girl was a torment to her own mother.' Normand sighed again; he had the right to. 'It doesn't matter this minute — it's something I'll have to anguish over. What should we do for now?'

'You'll have to bring her back over to your ranch,' Cougar said definitely. 'My wife's nerves are on edge, and I won't have that.'

'No. No, of course not. I can understand that. I'll have one of the men hitch the buckboard and we'll be over to your house within an hour.' He paused again before he asked, 'You were asking before about buying the black mare, Mr. Cougar. Would you still be interested?'

'No, sir. I don't think so. It just would not seem right somehow.'

Normand nodded and turned away toward the house, calling to someone within. Cougar stepped back into leather and turned the gray toward home pasture.

Gloria Fenner was taken away that morning, complaining and shouting a lot of unladylike curses by way of farewell. Cougar walked around the yard, clearing his mind, trying to plan ahead for a tomorrow which seemed far distant somehow.

He reflected again on how much trouble people put themselves through in order to be unhappy, then returned to the house for breakfast.

★ ★ ★

Tomorrow did come, of course.

The pantry was now fairly bulging with food. Cougar felt as if he were squandering his money, but he was not. He was just getting the stores up to where they should always have been. Living alone, he had paid little attention to these things except where the barest of necessities were involved. Everything was different with a woman in the house.

The roof was finally patched and the porch straightened up. He had dug the new well with the help of the younger Stroh brother, whom they now knew as Dan. It was Max Stroh who refused any work that did not have to do with horses. Dan was a willing worker, and much more cheerful once he was out of the shadow of his brooding brother. Once in a while Dan and Cougar would ride out to look at their small horse herd. The stallion had settled in enough so that it did not flee on their arrival.

'That little dun mare,' Dan announced with the experience of a horseman, 'she's coming into season. Wait and see if I'm not right. Your herd will be growing before long.'

Inside the house all was as it should be. The yellow pup was still as ungainly as ever, but Ellen had taught it its manners. The kitten had grown into a half-sized black cat. As far as Cougar knew it had never caught a rat yet, but it was eager to and was off like a shot at any sign of movement in the kitchen that he suspected.

They were both maturing into fine pets, and Cougar was thankful for that. Among other reasons was that when the baby arrived it would have a pair of animals to play with and to grow up with on the little ranch along Twin Creek.

Where Carroll and Ellen planned to live out their days. The cougar nevermore to prowling go.